ALL KINDS OF UGLY

ALL KINDS OF UGLY

RALPH DENNIS

ISBN-13: 978-1-941298-20-6

Published by
Brash Books, LLC
12120 State Line #253
Leawood, Kansas 66209
www.brash-books.com

PUBLISHER'S NOTE

Author Ralph Dennis died in 1988, leaving behind several unpublished manuscripts, including this one. *All Kinds of Ugly* was written in 1977 and is the long-lost, thirteenth and final novel in Ralph's acclaimed *Hardman* series. You can learn more about the manuscript, and its rediscovery, in the Afterword.

CHAPTER ONE

The dome on the State Capitol was gold-plated. From some figures I'd seen, gold was peeling and blowing away at the rate hundreds of dollars a day. With that much gold in the air, you'd think some state senator would spend his day standing downwind with his hat in his hands, trying to catch an ounce or so of it. No one did. There were other ways, easier ways, for a politician to fill his hat, and that's what Senator Arwine Black was doing.

He was on a committee that would be awarding an Atlanta contractor the deal to build a thirty mile stretch of highway south of Wilsonville. The contest was down to two firms: Dunlap & Brass and Coker Brothers. I was hired by a lobbyist for the Cokers to see if Senator Black had been bought by Dunlap & Brass with one or all of the three B's that were the coin of the realm: Booze, bread and broads.

For Senator Black, a portly man in his sixties with a wife, three kids, and four grandchildren, his price was broads. The younger the better.

An appointment was made for him by a Dunlap & Brass lobbyist through Claudia Marsh, a madam I knew. If you needed a one-legged whore, she could furnish one with three hours' notice. Claudia owed me some favors in exchange for some dirty work I'd done for her. All of my work was dirty since I'd left the Atlanta police force and started taking on odd jobs. This particular kind of work was the dirtiest, but it was easy, no felonies had to be committed, and my cash was running low. Claudia told me the girl, a thin red-head in her early twenties, was sent to a room at the West Peachtree Motor Hotel. That motel was, not-so-coincidentally, the one where Senator Black always kept a room when he was in Atlanta on state business.

I was parked across the street in my '65 Ford, ready-and-waiting and holding a rented camera with a telephoto lens, when Senator Black arrived in his Cadillac Eldorado. I snapped pictures as he was met at the door of the designated room by the red-head, who was dressed in a halter-top and denim shorts cut so short, it was almost possible to tell if she was a real red-head or not.

The door closed, and I was widening the frame when I saw a man I recognized emerging from the room next door. His name was Edward and I'd see him and my girl Marcy having dinner a few months back at Gene and Gabe's when I happened to be in the restaurant on a job. Edward was all the things I wasn't. He was my age, on the wrong side of forty, but without my paunch and with a golf course tan instead of my pale skin. He had a steady, nine-to-five job, probably read all the bestsellers, and had a favorite opera he could discuss at length. Marcy told me the dinner was just business with a colleague from the office.

Edward got into a gleaming new Mercury Montego and drove off. I took a few pictures of him, his car, and his license plate out of reflex. I looked back at the motel and noticed a blue Chevy Vega parked out front beside the empty space left by his Montego.

There were a lot of blue Vegas in Atlanta, but none with the small dent Marcy'd put on her rear bumper when she'd clipped my mailbox backing out my driveway a few months earlier.

I lingered, numb. A few minutes later, Marcy came out of the room. She was slim, blond, fine-boned and freshly showered, probably smelling of soap and the Charlie perfume I'd bought her last Christmas. I ducked down under the dash, my body across the passenger seat, so she wouldn't see me as she drove off.

I felt her standing outside the passenger door before she knocked on the window. I sat up, feeling guilty and stupid. Of course she'd recognized my car, even more easily than I'd spotted hers. There was a sad expression on her face.

She opened the door and got in. I was right. She did smell of soap and Charlie.

"How long have you been following me, Jim?"

"I wasn't. I'm on a job."

"That's what you said last time."

"It was true. Back then, you said you were having a business dinner."

"It was true, at the time. But you didn't believe me, so you started following me."

I'd felt her pulling away from me ever since that dinner, but we didn't talk about it and I didn't act on it. I knew what she'd wanted from me. She'd told me often enough over the years. A decent, regular job and a cleaner, safer life. I just couldn't bring myself to be the man she wanted and, despite her occasional tiffs, she'd seemed willing to settle for it.

I held up the rented camera. "I wouldn't need this to prove to myself what you're doing." For a moment, I wondered if maybe Edward was married, and Marcy thought I was taking photos to show his wife. "I'm following a Senator who likes young whores."

"You live in an ugly world."

"You're at this motel, too."

Her eyes flashed with anger. "Are you calling me a whore?"

"I'm saying we live in the same world."

She shook her head. "No, we don't. You live in one and I live in another. Yours is full of violence, crime and corruption. In some strange way, you and Hump are more comfortable there, moving in the darkness. I need to live in the light."

"Is that what meeting a guy in a motel for a lunch-time quickie is?"

Marcy didn't flinch. "Edward doesn't spend his days and nights in bars and strip clubs. His social circle isn't made up of drug dealers, thieves, mobsters, and prostitutes. He's never beaten or killed a man and he's never seen anybody die a violent death."

"He's been lucky."

"It's more than that. He isn't looking for any of it. You are. It's what you do and how you live."

I pointed to the motel. "The only thing that separates the two of you from the Senator and the whore in the room next door is a very thin wall. Maybe you didn't see them, or hear them, or you did and pretended you didn't, but they were there. In the same building, doing the same thing, but telling themselves different lies than you are telling yourselves. There is only one world, Marcy. You can hide behind walls. You can put in earplugs. You can cover your eyes and stomp your feet. But it's still there. Maybe I just don't like hiding, plugging my nose, or wearing a blindfold."

"I'm sorry for hurting you, Jim."

She turned and reached for the door handle.

"I just have one question," I said. "Why didn't you just end it with me instead of sneaking around?"

She looked back at me and wiped a tear from her cheek. "I'm the only light you have in your life and it's not easy to leave someone you love."

Marcy got out, walked over to her car, and drove off. I stuck around and to take a few more pictures of the Senator and the red-head when they left.

My house is twenty minutes outside of the city. I bought it during my first go-round with Marcy, back when I was still a cop, when I thought we might get married. That didn't happen and we broke up. I should have taken the hint the first time around, before she came back to Atlanta and to me and we repeated our mistakes.

The houses on my block are nicely painted and well-tended. Mine wasn't.

It needed a new paint job a decade before I bought it and the lawn was always overgrown. Every now and then one of my neighbors would cut my lawn as a gesture to keep the property values up. So far, none of them had offered to paint the house.

It was November and a day after I'd caught Marcy at the motel with the better version of me. I hadn't left the house and I'd been doing a lot of drinking. I smelled her everywhere.

Leaves were falling. I knew that when the weekend came, the neighbors on both sides of me would toil with rakes and plastic bags. And they'd bitch for the next few days that the leaves were blowing from my lawn onto theirs. Another no-win situation. I was an expert in no-win situations.

The leaves were a good burglar alarm. I heard someone kicking them around on my walkway. I sat up and reached for my trousers. I'd draped them over the back of a chair. I stepped into the legs, managed the zipper, and put my feet in my shoes without worrying about the laces. The knock came as I switched on a lamp.

Dapper Frank Butler stood on my narrow front porch. "You going to ask me in, Jim?"

"If I said no, you'd probably crawl in through my bedroom window."

"That's true." Frank was wearing a trench coat. He removed it and dropped it on one end of my sofa. He was wearing a soft gray plaid suit and a dark blue bow tie. The bow tie was his mark around town. "Have you been sick, Jim?"

I knew what he saw. The morning beard I'd scraped away with an electric razor was back and I was red-eyed from the half sleep. I was pale as a fish belly. "Only in the soul," I said.

"Ah," Frank said," I think we can find you a priest."

"How about a coffee instead?"

I left him in the living room and put on a kettle in my cramped kitchen. I found two clean cups and spooned in instant coffee. I waited for the water to boil. I occupied that time wondering what the hell Frank Butler was doing in my shack.

Butler used to be the real power in Atlanta until the blacks learned to vote in blocs and took his city away from him. If the loss of power bothered him, he hid it well.

"Milk or sugar, Frank?"

"One sugar."

I always believed the last ten years had been hard on him. His generation, the monied old upper class, felt they were under some oath to leave their city, their state, a better place than they found it. And now he sat back and watched the rednecks battle the blacks for political power. It made a sour world for him.

Butler sat on my rump-sprung sofa and carefully picked a wet leaf from the toe of one shoe. He accepted the coffee I placed in front of him. He sniffed it and his face revealed that he didn't quite trust instant coffee. He leaned forward and dropped the leaf into an ashtray.

"Does the name, Harrison Gault, mean anything to you, Jim?"

It did. A person didn't live long in Atlanta or in the state of Georgia without hearing the name from time-to-time. He'd been governor for one term back in the 1930's and he'd filled the remainder of a term as Senator when one of the incumbents died. But, against all urging, he refused to run for that office after he completed the term. He hated Washington. During an interview once he said that he had tried political power and it was overrated. What he did best was make money. He'd made a lot of it before he became old and sick. The last picture I'd seen of him he was like a dry twig, ready to break and fall away. He was in a wheelchair and he looked mad as hell about the shame of being seen that way.

"He has a grandson, Harrison Gault, the Third," Frank said. "They call him Harry and he is Harrison's only grand child and his heir."

There was more. Butler explained why Harry was the only heir. The old man's son and his wife, mother and father to the boy, had died in a plane crash when the boy was ten. It was a great blow to old Gault. As soon as he recovered from that loss he lavished everything he had on the little boy.

"How little?" I asked.

"Harry's in London now. He graduated from Harvard two years ago. He's at the London School of Economics now. I did my best to talk Harrison out of letting him go there. The whole faculty there is nothing but a band of Marxists."

"What's the problem?" I knew there had to be a problem or Frank Butler wouldn't subject himself to the germs in my house.

"He's missing. At least, he appears to be missing. His phone's been disconnected and a call I made to the London School indicates that he hasn't been to class this fall term."

"A dropout?"

Butler shook his head. "He's not the type."

"Letters from him?" I sipped my coffee. It was so bad it made cafeteria coffee sparkle and shine.

"Nothing since the middle of the summer."

"His bank?"

"A substantial check is deposited into his account each month at Barclay's on King's Road."

"But you don't know what, if anything, is happening with that account?"

"I called," Butler said. "British banks are very, very proper. They wouldn't tell me anything over the phone."

"The balance in the account?" I opened the end of a crushed package of Pall Mall's and lit one.

"Not that either."

"Interesting." I carried my coffee cup to the kitchen and poured the contents into the sink. I rinsed the cup. I found an orphan throwaway bottle of Bud in the refrigerator and twisted the cap. It hissed at me. "How does this ...?" I was almost shouting before I turned and saw that Butler had followed me to the kitchen doorway. "I mean, what does this have to do with me?"

"I was wondering if you were willing to make a trip to London. A week should do it."

"Why me?" I wasn't so modest I didn't know I had a few talents. I guess I wanted to know which ones of them Butler thought a job like this called for.

"This is a matter that needs to be handled with a certain delicacy and I was impressed with how you handled the Chambers business," he said.

Ellen Chambers was a wealthy woman who'd married a boy toy who played around with other women and did his best to steal her fortune. I'd put an end to it. It hadn't been pretty. Frank Butler was her lawyer. He represented a lot of rich people. Their money didn't insulate them from ugly problems.

"You have a passport?" Frank asked.

Getting away, far away, sounded like a good idea to me, even if I didn't like the job much that he was offering. "I think it expired last year."

"Simple enough. I can have it renewed for you."

He followed me through the living room and stopped in my bedroom doorway. The sheets and pillowcases needed changing.

The bed hadn't been made for days and one chair bottom was piled with dirty shirts and underwear. I rummaged around in the top dresser drawer until I found the passport. I leafed through it and carried it into the living room. I closed the bedroom door behind me. "How long ...?"

"Usually, it might take two weeks. I can shortcut that by a few days." He took my passport and shoved it in the pocket of his trench coat. "Harrison and I know some influential people at the State Department."

I got my Bud from the kitchen. The Pall Mall had tumbled from the ashtray to make another scar on the coffee table. "All expenses and pay for my time?"

"All expenses and a thousand a week."

"Generous," I said.

"What will you need?"

I thought about it for a few seconds. I sipped the Bud. "The round trip flights. Hotel reservations."

Butler nodded. He seemed impatient with me. "Of course, of course."

"The address of his apartment. A letter of introduction to someone at the London School of Economics. A letter to the boy's bank. You can make up some good reason why we need access to the boy's financial records."

"I'll work on something."

A wind blew leaves across the walkway. I could hear the scuttle and scratch. "The expense money in front."

"You'll have it." He stood and struggled into his trench coat. "I appreciate this, Jim."

I considered asking him why he didn't make the trip himself. He would have some answer that made sense. The real truth was that his time was gold. He didn't spend it looking around London for the grandson of a friend. "That's all right. I need a vacation anyway."

CHAPTER TWO

Eight days later, with my renewed passport, I boarded the Delta flight from Hartsfield to London. Frank Butler, as if to remind me that I was an employee, had booked me into coach.

Two days before I left, I finally told Hump about Marcy, but he'd figured it out on his own. He said the tell wasn't how much I was drinking, but the way I was doing it.

He'd know. I did most of my drinking with him. Eating, too. He was six-six, two-hundred and seventy pounds, and black as coal. He'd been an NFL defensive end until he tore up his knee. An operation put the knee back together, but pro ball was out and he didn't like coaching pay. He discovered he could make more as hired muscle. When he needed money, and I needed a back-up man, I gave him a call. Always a fifty-fifty split.

Art Maloney, my old partner when I was a cop, heard about the split with Marcy from his wife Edna, who was friends with her. He came down to see me at George's Deli and yelled at me for ruining it with her. I guessed Marcy'd didn't share the circumstances of our break-up and I didn't tell him. I didn't see any reason to ruin her image. Mine was already beyond repair, so I could take the extra smear.

It was a Sunday when I arrived in London. The hotel I'd been booked into was a middle of the road place. Not for the wealthy and not for the tour groups, either. After a nap, I showered and sat on the edge of the bed and tried to plan my week. Sunday. The bank wouldn't be open. I'd have to wait until the following morning for that. Nothing I could do about the London School of Economics, either. That left the last address Harry Gault had given his grandfather. Smith Street. I'd bought a London Street guide. A few minutes of eye strain and I found the street. In the Chelsea section. It ran into King's Road. I dressed and put on my trench coat, a new purchase for the trip. Everybody seemed to wear one when they went to England. Why should I be different?

Smith was a street hardly two blocks long. At one end of it was King's Road. At the other end, it butted into the main entrance of The Royal Hospital, the retirement home for military men. In the first block, after the turn from King's Road, there were flats on both sides of the street and at least one pub. I read the pub sign as the taxi passed. The Phoenix. The left side of the second block was an enclosed field or athletic park. On the right was a row of flats.

"Should be about here, sir," the cabbie said.

I paid him and stepped out into the weather. The wind was raw. I didn't know it at the time, but I was close to the Embankment of the Thames. Perhaps that was why it seemed damp and cold. Or it was the usual London weather for the time of year.

The taxi pulled away. I crossed the street. Halfway down the row, I found the street number I was looking for. It took me a little longer to find Flat #1. It turned out to be the basement apartment. There was a name card tacked to the door but the weather had washed the writing from it. I couldn't find a doorbell. I stepped forward and whapped the door a couple of times with the heel of my hand.

A minute passed. I heard locks, three or four of them, and then the door was opened a crack. I looked down into a black face. A man with his hair done in dreadlocks, the Rastafarian hairdo.

"I don't know you, mon. Why you hammering on me door?"

"I'm looking for Harry Gault. This is the last address…"

"Do I have the look of your Harry Gault?" He started to edge the door closed.

"It's important," I said.

"You're not a Brit?"

"American," I said. "Can we get out of the wind?" I shivered. It was a real shiver.

He swung the door wide and let me inside. The room was bare, hardly furnished at all. There were a couple of chairs and a table that was probably used for dining. Straight ahead, past the room we were in, there was a narrow hallway and a closed door. The room was cold. A single electric space heater hummed and heated a small area a couple of feet directly in front of it. I thought I could hear, from beyond the closed door, the muffled sound of reggae played on a cheap hi-fi system.

"I thought you were a copper," the man with the dreadlocks said.

"Not very likely," I said. I looked around the room. I moved over and stood near the space heater. "How long have you lived here?"

"Since August."

"You ever meet the Harry Gault I asked about?"

"Not really. Some of his things were here when I moved in. The next day, a couple come by for them."

"A man and woman?"

He nodded.

"How could you be sure the man wasn't Harry Gault?"

"He was an American, wasn't he? These two were foreign."

"How's that?"

"A man and woman with strange accents. I don't know which country they were from. A young girl with dark hair, with what they call the body of a peasant. A large woman." He smiled, as if to indicate he liked big women.

"The man?"

"Short and thin. He had a dark kind of white skin."

"You get their names?"

"I don't think they give me names," he said,

I backed away from the space heater. I'd been close enough to smell the cloth of my trousers begin to burn. "How did they haul his things away?"

"There was a taxi at the curb."

"You moved in when ... exactly?"

"The middle of August."

It was, I thought, about as much as I was going to get. I had a time frame. I buttoned my trench coat and decided I'd buy a scarf and a cap the next day. I headed for the outside door. I was almost there when the door at the other end of the narrow hall opened. I turned. Another black man, this one thick and heavy in the chest and with the same dreadlocks, stood in the hallway with about the biggest joint of grass I'd ever seen. It was a big as a cigar. He puffed and smoked obscured his face. The man saw me through it and backed away and closed the door with a loud slam.

"It is part of our religion," the little dark man explained.

"Cool," I said. "It's cool with me." I smiled and he smiled and then he let me out of the flat.

I walked down Smith Street, headed for King's Road. By my watch, it was a couple of minutes after one in the afternoon. I stopped across the street from the Phoenix pub. My stomach growled at me. With the jet lag, I didn't know which meal of the day I'd missed.

I'd brought along a dozen rolls of Tums just in case foreign food didn't agree with me. An unopened roll was in my right-hand coat pocket.

I crossed the street and entered the Phoenix. It wasn't what I'd expected from a public house. It was more like an American bar. There was a juke box mounted in one wall and central heating and a pool table in the back room. I got a pint of bitter from the bar and looked in the front room. The steam table there was dark and covered. No food served, it seemed, on Sunday.

I carried my pint into the back room. I watched the pool game in progress. The bitter took some getting used to. For my tongue, it had a taste like dirty dishwater smelled. I sat at a small table to the left of the pool table. There was a bowl of salted peanuts there, next to the ashtray. I nibbled at them and watched the match underway.

One of the shooters, the one with the long blond hair and the beach bum look, was English. The other was American and from his accent, from somewhere in the mid-west. On the far side of the pool table, there were eight or ten young men waiting their turn at the table and there was a slate with names chalked on it.

A possibility came to me. This was the closest pub to the flat young Gault had rented. It was a longshot, but because it was also in the American style, have been one of his watering places.

The pool shoot wound down. The English boy routed the one I'd tagged as being from the mid-west. When the American put his stick away, he picked up a jacket with DePaul across the back of it and sat at the table on my right.

"American, aren't you?" I said. "I've been trying to place the accent."

"Kansas City," the young man said.

I nodded. "Atlanta."

He watched the break. I was bothering him.

"You a regular here?"

"Some."

"You know another American who used to come here? His name was Harry Gault."

He kept his eyes on the pool match. "I knew one Harry. I didn't get his last name. I think he was over at L.S.E."

It took me a few moments to translate that into London School of Economics. I had a recent picture of Harry Gault in my pocket. I didn't like to show pictures. It got people uptight, considering their answers and wondering who the hell was asking the questions and why. "You know him well?"

The Kansas City toy wasn't dumb. He made his leap without having the photo shown to him. "You asking these questions for any special reasons?"

"I'm a family friend. His granddaddy asked me to look in on him while I'm here. The only problem is that he's moved and I don't have a forwarding address."

He chewed that a time. It must have gone down easy. "To tell the truth, I've hardly seen him all summer. Maybe…" He turned his head away from me and looked into the crowded barroom. "You telling the truth?"

"Cross my heart. And I don't have a lot of time to chase him all over London."

"I'll chance it," he said. He got to his feet and looked down at me. "There's a girl here. I think I saw her in there a few minutes ago."

I watched him go. I slugged away at the pint of bitter. He was gone a time and just when I'd decided it was a game, and that he'd left, I saw some people at the edge of a crowd part and he returned. He had a pretty dark-haired girl with delicate skin in tow. She might have been a model or a movie star. That was until she opened her mouth and I saw her teeth. They were crooked and some were discolored.

"This is Heddy." The Kansas City boy picked up his glass and began to back away. "She said she'll talk to you."

I introduced myself. I motioned her into a seat at my table. The boy nodded at me and circled the pool table. Using a nub of chalk, he wrote his name on the slate board. Heddy carried one of those small half-pint jugs. It was empty.

"What are you having? Let me get us another one."

"The cider on draft," she said.

"I'll try that myself." I elbowed my way to the bar and bought two pints of cider. I returned to the table and eased into a seat next to her. "I don't know how much he told you, Heddy…"

"He said you were looking for Harry."

I caught the Irish accent then, soft and pleasant. Being Irish probably explained the crooked, discolored teeth. The Irish had never been big on dentists. "You know him?"

"Yes. You see, I work here Tuesday and Thursday nights."

"How well do you know him?"

"We've been to films and plays and for drinks."

"Good friends?"

She blushed and covered herself by lifting the pint and gulping the cider. When she lowered the glass, she said, "Yes." The blush faded into the pale skin.

I told her my tale. The reason for my search for Harry Gault. I had to admit to myself that it got better and better the more I told it.

"It's odd you should be looking for him here," Heddy said.

"At this pub? That was a lucky accident. You see, I was…"

"No." She shook her head. "Here in England. The last I heard from him, he was going back to the States."

The best Heddy remembered, it had been the first week in August. A Tuesday night, she thought. She was working behind the bar and it was a busy night for a Tuesday. Harry had called and she'd had little time to talk to him. The next night, Wednesday, they were supposed to go to a film. Harry called to say that he had to break the date. In fact, it was more than that. Harry said there was an illness in his family at home, in the States, and he was trying to arrange a flight for the next day. "He said he'd call me as soon as he returned."

"Did he?"

She shook her head. "If he returned at all. I don't know that he did."

There was hurt in her, layered over, but still there. The relationship, I guessed, was more than a simple friendship. I suspected that she took his sudden leaving as a rejection of her, a way of freeing himself.

"No letters?"

"No."

I think she'd told me all that she knew. A dark Irishman with a swagger and a scowl came to the doorway of the back room where the pool table was. He stared at me and at Heddy. She said a hurried goodbye and left my table. He met her at the doorway and grabbed her arm. Before a new record began on the juke box, I thought I heard a sharp remark from the dark Irishman and a protest from her. They turned and merged into the crowded bar and were gone.

I drank most of the pint of cider. Before I left, I caught the eye of the Kansas City boy and waved at him. He returned the wave. I walked the block to King's Road before I found a taxi.

CHAPTER THREE

The next morning, a taxi dropped me in front of the Barclay's Bank on King's Road. Before I went inside, I looked around. It was a small world, I decided. The entrance to Smith Street was a block behind me. Harry Gault had selected a bank near his flat.

It was windy and there was a cold sun. The sidewalks were jammed in this section of King's Road with the punk people. Young boys and girls in outrageous combinations of clothing. Some of them had short hair, with the edges of it dyed blue and red and yellow. While I stood on the sidewalk in front of the bank, a couple passed me. The young man wore an ankle length leather coat and held a leash in his hand. His girl was two paces behind him, the leash attached to a wide dog collar she wore around her neck.

One thing about English banks. They didn't intend to get robbed often. It was a bulletproof glass world inside Barclay's. There was a metal speaking tube at the head level. At the counter level, it was a system of drawers that moved checks and money back and forth between the customers and the teller inside.

I reached the head of a line after a five-minute wait. "I need to see the manager," I told the teller.

"You wish to start an account?"

"I wish to see the manager," I said.

The teller left the window for a few seconds. When she returned, she said, "Mr. Dalrymple will be with you directly."

I stepped aside. I turned. There was a door behind me. I heard it open, followed by the snick of the lock. After the door closed, a man held out his hand to me.

"You wish to see me?"

I touched the soft hand and released it. I put his age at around forty. A dark, well-cut suit. He had the ruddy face of a man who spent a lot of time in the sun when he could find it. Or the coloring could have been from walking too much in the London weather.

I passed Frank Butler's letter to him. It was sealed but I had read the letter at the law office when we had our last meeting to go over the game plan.

The banker, Mr. Dalrymple, looked at the seal. I think he regretted that he hadn't brought a letter opener with him. He tapped the letter and tore away one end of the envelope.

I watched Mr. Dalrymple read the letter. It was on the fancy law firm letterhead. In the letter, Butler wrote that he had been authorized to look into the financial affairs of Mr. Harrison Gault, the Third. This task had been assigned to him by the young man's grandfather, Harrison Gault, Senior. Enclosed, Barclay's would find a notarized statement from Mr. Harrison Gault, Senior to this effect. The law firm's representative, Mr. Jim Hardman, should be offered all such courtesies that would be extended to family or to the law firm by the bank.

Mr. Dalrymple finished his reading. He blew softly into the end of the envelope and inserted the letter and the notarized statement. "I regret that I do not understand what Mr ...."

"Butler," I said.

"... expects of Barclay's."

"I think Mr. Butler expects me to audit young Gault's bank account so that we can see what the lad has been up to."

"I'm afraid our bank..."

"These are not ordinary circumstances. The boy's grandfather believes the boy is in some kind of trouble."

"I would suggest the police ..."

"We hope it is not that kind of trouble. There is a suspicion that the young man is being victimized by someone who ... well.

let's say it is a matter of increased expenses. While Mr. Gault is generous with his grandson, he is not about to be made a fool of by anyone."

It was touch-and-go and then touch-and-go again. I could feel the banker waver. I decided to push him over the line.

"Mr. Gault and his lawyer understand that there is an ethical problem here, that the bank had certain obligations to its clients. At the same time, we believe that our request is within the boundaries of propriety. Each month a draft is deposited into the account of young Mr. Gault. This bank draft comes from his grandfather. Mr. Harrison Gault, Senior has every right to know what happens to *his* funds."

"Let me take your coat."

I removed my trench coat and handed it to Mr. Dalrymple. It was, I realized later, his way of making sure that I didn't carry a weapon into the enclosed part of the bank. He stepped past me and spoke to the teller at the nearest window.

When we reached the locked door, there was an electronic buzz, the door was unlocked and we entered the banking fortress.

I'd thought it might take an hour. It hardly took twenty minutes. All the checks were from the old batch, imprinted with the Smith Street address. That was no help. But there were few checks for the month so far. There was a single deposit to the account, from First Georgia in Atlanta, for two thousand dollars.

Dalrymple furnished me a desk and a pen and a pad. That done, he settled into a desk nearby. In fact, I had the feeling that he was observing me the whole time. To be certain, I thought, that I didn't get within feet of any of the money.

I put the checks in order.

On November 1st, there was a check to Alistair Parks and Associates for two hundred pounds, A note at the bottom of the check explained it. *Rent.*

I noted Alistair Parks. I could find him later in the phone book and get an address.

There were other odds and ends. A twenty-pound check here and there. Cashed at this pub or that one. At a food market, at a fruitier, at a butcher shop. I put those check aside. No utility bills but I'd heard those bills were sent out quarterly and it was probably the wrong month.

I was left with two checks written out to Miss Anna Piroski. Each check was for a hundred and fifty pounds. One on November 8th and the other on November 15th.

I drew the desk calendar toward me. The 8th was a Wednesday and so was the 15th. By my estimate, today was the 20th, a Monday. I'd hardly turned in my chair when Dalrymple appeared beside me.

I passed the two checks to him, the ones written to Anna Piroski. "What can you tell me about these?"

He studied the checks. He turned them in his hands. "A moment, please."

I watched him stride down the line of tellers. He stopped at the far end, next to a plump, elderly lady with gray hair. He leaned over her, they talked for a time, and then he nodded and backed away.

"Most of our clients prefer to deal with the same tellers," he said.

I nodded. I understood that. I'd done the same in Atlanta until I realized that as soon as I got to know one of the tellers, she always got pregnant and left. Then I'd have to start all over with another teller.

"Mrs. Featherstone remembers that young lady. A girl in her twenties. Dark hair. A small mole on her chin. Mrs. Featherstone believes she is European. Hungarian or Slovak or Polish. For the last three months or so this young woman comes in every Wednesday and cashes a check for this same amount. She always asks for it in ten-pound notes."

"What time does she usually come in?"

Dalrymple fought irritation. "I'll ask." He had a few words with Mrs. Featherstone and returned. "Usually at ten in the morning."

I wrote down Miss Anna Piroski on the pad and tore the sheet away. I returned the pad, the pen and the stack of checks to Mr. Dalrymple. "There's never any question about cashing these checks for this Piroski woman?"

"The account is solvent, the young woman has identification and the signature is authentic."

"Or appears to be," I said.

He gave me a stern look. "Are you quite done?"

I said I was. He followed me to the door and, after the door was open and I was through it, he passed me my trench coat. I thanked him for his trouble.

He mumbled something about it being highly irregular, the whole business.

Alistair Parks and Associates was in a second-floor office on Beauchamp Place. Downstairs, on the street level, there was an iron frame that held tile-like signs, rental listings for the week.

"And you're not here to rent or to purchase?" The slim, blonde lady had been all warmth, the charm that I guess all Americans expect after having watched too much BBC television on the educational channels. Then I'd asked about Harry Gault and she wasn't charming anymore. "I am certain it is not in our interests to give out such information. I have only your word that you have any connection to Mr. Gault."

I stood. The chair hadn't been comfortable anyway and I was glad I hadn't bothered to remove my trench coat. "I suppose it's the police then. Something irregular is going on and the police might be our only hope." Mentally I thanked Mr. Dalrymple for "irregular." It was a good word. At the same time, I noticed that, from the time I got off the plane at Heathrow. I'd started to talk in a stilted way, as if I had hopes of being accepted at Oxford.

"I'm sure I don't know what you mean."

"I believe you might answer these same questions if the police were asking them."

"*If* the police were asking them." She nodded.

"I fail to understand why you can't give me the address of the grandson of an old …"

"He has the right of privacy. He is of age, isn't he?"

I agreed that he was.

"I'll make one effort," the lady said. "If you'll leave me your name and where you're staying here in London, I'll talk to Mr. Gault. He can decide at that time whether he wishes to speak with you."

It was as far as she was going to go. I wrote my name and the name of the hotel on the pad she offered me. She turned the pad and I thought I saw her nose wrinkle slightly when she identified the hotel. Frank Butler hadn't spent any money trying to help my credibility.

I had lunch at The Bunch of Grapes, a pub on Brompton. I had a Cornish something that was like a popover but it was filled with some kind of shredded meat and potatoes and I had French fries which they called "chips" and the baked beans that weren't really more than pork and beans without any of the special flavorings that I expected in baked beans.

On the street again, the heavy weight of the lunch dragging at me, I reached for my first roll of Tums and opened it. I sucked on two Tums. I hoped I'd brought enough tablets to last a week. I didn't think the job would last longer than that.

The American Embassy was like an armed camp. All briefcases and packages were searched. I had to walk through a metal detector. Marine guards watched all arrivals with a no-nonsense attitude.

I sent in the name Frank Butler had given me. After a time, a young woman came for me. A Marine guard passed me from his care into hers and I followed her deep into the bowels of the building. The girl led me into his office and backed away. I turned and watched her seat herself behind a reception desk.

Miles Carson was lean and pale and just past thirty. He talked like he still had a mouthful of spoonbread. South Carolina, I thought. Given the time, I might even have been able to pick the county he was from.

I told him the results of my search so far.

He nodded. "I had a telex from State. You seem to carry some clout with you."

"Not me. Harrison Gault."

He whistled. "That old bastard still alive?"

"He was when I left Atlanta."

"Then he still is. They say he's too mean to die and make half the state of Georgia happy."

While I was talking, he'd made notes. Now he picked up a gold Mark Cross pen and drew a line under Anna Piroski. "Polish, you think?"

"Sounds that way."

"Let's try a long shot," Carson said. He walked to the office doorway "Donna, see if there's an immigration application for a Miss Anna Piroski." He spelled out the last name slowly.

"Might be something in the *Wants To* file." After her heel taps faded in the distance Carson eased himself into the seat behind his desk once more. "The Brits have a hell of an immigration problem. You read about the race riots all the way over there in the States?"

I nodded.

"We tend to think of the people who flood England as being from India or from the Caribbean. But there are a lot of Europeans as well, Poles, for example. They come over on a limited work visa. Say one year. Once they're here, they spend that year trying to find a way to stay."

"For example?"

"Marriage to a British citizen. That's the easy one. Say a Polish girl wants to remain in England. She finds herself a poof..." Carson hesitated. "You know what a poof is?"

I said I didn't.

"A homosexual. Probably some kid in a red brick university who needs the money. The Polish girl pays the poof two or three hundred pounds and they get married. They never live together. And the Brit immigration doesn't hassle them the way they do the blacks who try to work the same business. But back to the Polish girl. A year after the wedding... the girl's not under a work visa now because she's married to a citizen... they get a divorce. The girl pays for this too. The poof goes back to university. The girl's in for good and all's well that ends well. Hell, there are probably a lot of divorced Polish virgins out there in the city of London."

I laughed.

"Well, maybe not," Miles Carson said. "But it's possible in the best of worlds."

His secretary, Donna, returned. She leaned across the desk and placed a folder in from of him. Carson smiled. "I think I'll take up fortune telling." Then he smiled modestly. "It really wasn't more than a good guess. Early on, these people who don't want to return home try to use England as a stepping stone. To the States, usually. The drawback is that they don't usually have any kind of profession that gives them priority in the yearly quota." He opened the folder and read the top page, nodding to himself.

"You going to tell me what's in Anna Piroski's file?"

"I can't do that." Miles Carson puffed himself into a righteous pose. "That would be a violation of the privacy act that the State Department subscribes to. Letting you see this document would be a real no-no." He stood. "I've got to go to the loo. I'll be gone about two minutes. I want to stress to you that you are not to touch this file while I'm gone."

"You've got my promise."

He closed the door behind him. I grabbed the file and opened it. It was a standard form. I didn't have time to read all of it. What I wanted was an address. I found one. *112 Burnam Court.* I wrote that on a scrap of paper. Under professions: *seamstress, waitress and housekeeper.* Not a brain surgeon or an architect after all.

Skimming it quickly. Sponsor: *Harrison Gault.* That stopped me until I saw the address given. Not the old man. The grandson. Harrison Gault, the sponsor, lived on Smith Street and listed himself as a graduate student and an American citizen.

The door knob rattled a time or two. I closed the file and placed it where it had been. I'd just settled my butt into a seat again when Miles Carson entered.

"Now you didn't read the Piroski file, did you?"

I said I hadn't.

"A good man, an honorable man," Carson said.

"Doesn't live here anymore." The frumpy little woman in the doorway wore a stained housedress and, over that, what looked like a canvas apron.

Burnam Court was gray and bleak under a dark sky. It was probably gray and bleak when the sun was out. I nodded at the lady and cleaned the soles of my shoes on the iron scraper to the left of her door. Somewhere, between the cab and her stoop, I'd stepped into some dog crap.

"No reason to be doing that," the woman said. "You're not being asked in." A smell of boiling cabbage drifted past her on the soggy air that came from inside her flat.

"How long ago did Miss Piroski leave?"

"Long after she was welcome," the woman said.

"When?"

"Early in August I think it was."

That fitted into the time frame I'd put together.

"Her and that rabble of hers. Drinking and dancing and chanting all night."

"Chanting?"

"It was a strange tongue the words were in."

Probably Polish. "You know where Miss Piroski moved?"

Her mouth was twisted and sour. "Wherever it is, it's not quiet there anymore." With that, the woman backed away and closed the door in my face.

Tuesday morning. There was a thunderstorm in my head. With nothing better to do with my time, I'd done a night prowl of several pubs. In one place, late at night, a redhead I'd bought a couple of drinks for had "allowed as how" she'd sleep with me if I'd pay her fifty pounds. I'd said, right back, that I'd sleep with her if she'd pay me twenty pounds.

"You'd not that bloody handsome," she hissed at me and stomped away.

I wasn't bloody handsome at all. Maybe if I'd set my price lower. At ten pounds?

I had breakfast in the hotel dining room. When I returned to the lobby, the desk clerk called to me. There was a message from the woman at Alistair Parks and Associates on Beauchamp Place. I used the house phone to return the call.

"They don't want to see you," the lady said.

"They? Did you talk to Harry Gault?"

"Not directly," the lady said. "I spoke with a lady who said she was relaying a message from Mr. Gault."

"I see." I don't know why I said that. I didn't see. "She give her name?"

"I didn't ask. I assume she is the woman I've spoken with several times before."

"Which woman is that?"

"You know how young people are these days. No morals at all. I believe she is the woman Mr. Gault lives with."

"Have you talked to Mr. Gault recently?"

"Not since he rented the flat. But I understand he is quite busy with his studies at the London School of Economics."

"And there is no way I can get the address from you?"

"I fear not."

I told her she hadn't been any help at all. For some reason, she got huffy then and hung up the phone on me.

Later that morning, I placed a call to Barclay's on King's Road. Mr. Dalrymple wasn't in. He was home with a cold and fever. The receptionist was not willing to give me his home phone number. I asked to talk to someone else, another management type. She said she would connect me with Mr. Forbes.

Forbes heard most of my story. I could feel the shock waves travel through the wires.

"That is not proper," Forbes said. "There is no circumstance under which I can give you the address of a client."

To hell with it. Tomorrow would be Wednesday and, if nothing changed, Anna Piroski would make her weekly pilgrimage to Barclay's with her check for a hundred and fifty pounds.

I'd be on her like a wet postage stamp.

Frank Butler called that evening when I was about to leave the hotel and find a place for supper. I'd spent the afternoon walking around London, being a tourist. It would have been fun with Marcy. Or even Hump. Alone, it was dull and endless. I was tired and leg weary and windburned.

"What's going on over there, Jim? How's your vacation?"

I sat on the edge of the bed. A steam radiator tinkled away across the room from me.

"With any luck I'll know something tomorrow."

"How does it look?"

"It's got a bad feeling to it," I said. "In fact, it stinks."

Butler wanted me to elaborate on that but I ducked and dodged. Maybe I was wrong. If I was, there was no reason to worry the folks in Atlanta. Still, there were too many walls up, no straight talk, and all I'd found so far were dead end streets and alleys.

"Call me whatever hour it is," Butler said. He even gave me his unlisted phone number at home.

I said I would. After the call ended, I stood at the window and watched the dark hood of night sky settle over London.

I was outside Barclay's the next morning when the doors opened for business. I didn't see Mr. Dalrymple anywhere beyond the fortress of glass. Perhaps he was still at home with his cold and fever.

I stood at a counter against the wall and doodled over some forms in the pigeonholes there. I think I applied for automatic overdraft and for guaranteed check cashing. I was starting over on a new automatic overdraft application when the door opened behind me. A blast of cold wind pushed at me and a group of people entered, blowing on their hands and stomping their feet.

There was a short line at the teller window near me. Two men and three women lined up there. The longest line was at the far end, at the window where Mrs. Featherstone was. About eight people in all there. I caught a scent of some kind of perfume and then a woman brushed past me and headed for the longer teller line.

I hadn't talked to Mrs. Featherstone but I knew she remembered me. I'd considered asking her to give me some indication when Anna Piroski arrived. It turned out it wasn't necessary. As soon as the women who brushed past me joined the line in front of her, Mrs. Featherstone lifted her head and looked at me.

From the back, Anna looked stocky and heavy. A strong back and athletic legs. She wore a long gray wool coat. I could see the ends of dark hair curling from beneath a print scarf she wore over her head.

I passed her and entered the foreign exchange room. I turned and had a look at her. A pleasant face, attractive enough, wide cheekbones and gray eyes. Before she became aware of my stare, I walked to the exchange window and cashed a couple of hundred dollar traveler's checks. Anna was still in the line when I passed the doorway. I walked outside and crossed King's Road. I found a doorway there and stood out of the wind and waited. After five minutes or so, Anna Piroski left the bank, buttoning her coat and turning up her collar, and turned to her left. She headed in the direction of the Smith Street intersection. I gave her a twenty-yard head start and then followed. We were like that, on opposite sides of the wide street, for about a long block.

At the Smith Street intersection, Anna joined two or three other people and crossed King's Road. She was headed directly for me. I stopped and put my back to her and studied a group of tweed jackets in a men's shop window. When I turned, I thought Anna had headed down Smith Street. She hadn't. She'd crossed Smith Street, still on King's Road. I followed. She passed a couple of men's clothing shops, an open courtyard and a butcher shop. She paused and I saw her reach into her purse. I watched her as she moved into a doorway. I stopped at the butcher store and stared at still-feathered pheasant hanging in the window.

I waited about a minute. Then I moved slowly past the doorway where I'd last seen Anna Piroski. A light flared on in a shop there. It as a Dayville's Ice Cream Parlor, and it seemed to be patterned after Baskin-Robbins. Or perhaps it was the other way around.

There was a raised platform area at the back of the Parlor. There were tables and chairs there and a coat rack. Anna had just removed her heavy coat. She wore a serving uniform. A blue dress and a frilly white apron. Her head was down while she adjusted a cap on her head. I had my look at her body. Full breasted and a narrow waist, a flaring of wide hips. And when she lifted her head, I saw the full, almost petulant mouth.

I found a hole in the traffic and crossed the street. I stood in front of a bakery and watched the doorway of the Dayville Parlor. There was a smell of fresh bread in the warm air vented from the basement grate at the street level.

I shivered and asked myself how long her shift was. I hoped it wasn't eight hours.

At eleven exactly the large pub, The Drug Store, opened two doors down from Dayville's. The next hour was a slow one. It wasn't the season for ice cream.

I considered going in for a cone and a few minutes of warmth. I might have if there'd been enough business in Dayville's so there was a chance I might blend in. During the first hour and a half, I counted three customers. Not enough cover, I decided. I didn't want to draw attention to myself. Not yet. So, I shifted from frozen foot to frozen foot and watched the King's Road circus pass by.

At noon, Anna Piroski opened the door and backed out. She bent over the lock. I watched her turn toward the Drug Store. She mounted the steps and entered the pub. I waited until the door closed behind her. I angled across the street and looked at Dayville's locked door. There was a sign behind the glass. CLOSED FOR LUNCH.

I entered the pub. It was a huge room. To the right was a bar that was almost a hundred feet long. On the left was a steam counter. Anna Piroski was near the front of the line. There were two women behind her. I hid myself behind the two of them and watched while Anna ordered a tomato and cheese sandwich on brown bread. Anna moved away, toward the bar, and I read the menu and kept my head turned away from her. There was one item listed on the menu that caught my attention. Plowman's

Lunch. I didn't know what that was. When my time came, when I reached the head of the line, I ordered it. It turned out to be a length of French bread, a slab of Cheddar cheese and some pickled onions and a pat of butter.

I found a seat at the bar that was two stools down from where Anna sat. The bartender, who'd been laughing and joking with Anna, took my order for a pint of bitter. After he drew it, he made change and moved away. He leaned toward Anna and said something I didn't hear. Anna swung on her bar stool and looked at me and they laughed together. I raised an eyebrow at them.

The bartender moved into the space between Anna and me. "No offense," he said. "I was joking. I said you didn't look like a plowman."

"I'm not." I smiled. "I guess I've always wanted to know what a plowman has for lunch."

Anna watched me with steady, gray eyes. "American?"

I said I was.

"Which city or state are you from?" Her English was stiff and awkward.

"Miami, Florida," I said.

"Ah." She bit a huge chunk from her sandwich. It was washed down with a swallow from a half pint jug. "It is always warm there?"

"Usually," I said.

Anna was pleased. She nodded to herself like she'd just passed an examination. At that moment, as if I'd willed it, a man dressed in coveralls splattered with plaster sat on the stool between Anna and me. She appeared to lose interest in me and in Miami. I ate my lunch, buttering chunks of the French bread and eating them with slices of cheese.

I'd pushed the plate away when I heard chair legs scrape. Anna was headed for the front door. When she was level with me her step slowed. She stopped and touched me on the shoulder. "Miami? Is that city near Atlanta?"

"About the distance from here to Scotland," I said.

"That distant?"

I nodded.

She left. I pushed the dregs of the pint of bitter aside and ordered a double scotch. I poured it back and went outside again. The scotch glowed in the pit of my stomach.

I was uneasy about the encounter with Anna in the pub. It was the last thing I wanted, to be noticed. I had a feeling this girl was no dumb Polish joke.

I made short visits to the pub all afternoon. By four the sky was dark. By five it was almost night. At five-fifteen a young man in a threadbare tweed coat entered the Dayville's Parlor. A few minutes later, Anna left the shop and stood under the awning while she buttoned her coat. She looked left and right and thought I felt her eyes brush over me. A flick and a lock on me.

I knew I was right when she slung her purse strap over her shoulder and crossed King's Road. The angle brought her toward me. I stamped my feet to restore some feeling in them and stared at the sidewalk. I saw the toes of her boots first.

"Miami? I do not believe you."

I lifted my head and looked into the gray eyes. "Would I lie to you?"

A curl of her mouth. Almost a smile. "Are you one of those nasty men who follow young girls?"

"That's it."

"You are not a handsome man. You are not ugly either. You could take me to dinner some night."

"Tonight?"

"Not tonight." There was a hesitation before she spoke again. "Miami, have you ever been to a Polish wedding?"

"No. And you can call me Jim."

"The wedding is over. This is the wedding party. Would you like to come?"

It was getting to me. I was being vamped. Her eyes almost fluttering. And I could feel the earthiness of her. "Sure," I said. "I'd like to come."

"Miami, you have to bring presents. It is expected."

"What kind of presents?"

"If you have money, you should bring Polish vodka."

I nodded. "All right."

"Are you rich, Miami?"

"As rich as most Americans are."

"Ah," Anna said, "then I will like you."

CHAPTER FOUR

Anna led me down a dark walk. It was a sort of narrowed in courtyard. Small flats on both sides. The scent of dank earth seemed to swirl around us. I couldn't smell Anna's perfume anymore.

I carried the Polish vodka and the wine. She'd picked three bottles of some brand I'd never heard of and I selected three bottles of a medium-priced Claret. I'd paid for it and it hadn't seemed much until I remembered I was paying in pounds and not dollars.

The closed end of the courtyard was straight ahead. A dim yellow bulb burned over the door. While Anna fumbled for her key I listened to the music. Loud and scratchy records. Polish music or gypsy music or whatever. It was being played on a turntable that dragged, slipped, or on an old windup Victrola that was two or three turns from winding down.

"She is my best friend," Anna said. "We have been friends since we were children."

"Who?"

"The bride. We call her Mitka."

She inserted the key and we entered. Anna yelled something over the music. In Polish, I thought. Then she turned and I passed the bag of bottles to her. "Vodka," she said, holding up the first bottle of clear liquid. The second and then the third.

We'd entered a shabby living room. It was painted the color of lightly creamed coffee. There were chairs along the walls to the left and right and a large table in the center of the room. I saw three opened bottles of cheap red wine, a plate of some kind of dark sausage and crackers and a large bowl of wrapped penny candies.

I counted three women and three men. The men were swarthy and slight, wiry and unshaven. They looked at Anna as if she were the Queen of the Gypsies. The stares I got from them were questioning and hostile. Even when Anna explained, in English for my benefit, that the vodka was my wedding present, I felt only a slight relaxation of the tension. The reception for the vodka, however, was friendly enough. One of the women clapped her hands together, laughed, and ran into the kitchen. She returned with a tray of glasses of different shapes and sizes. The tumbler I got was still damp and greasy to the touch. Anna opened the first bottle and poured for the women first, then for me and herself, and passed the rest of the bottle to one of the men who sat at the table.

No one drank until Anna said something in Polish and added, in English, "This is my American friend, Miami."

We drank. All at the same time. Bottoms up and not a drop left in any glass.

The bottle passed between the three Polish men and women guests. Anna stood close to me and smiled. "I do like you, Miami. I will show you my room later."

I removed my trench coat and placed one of the bottles of Claret on top of it. "For later," I said.

"Yes." She still smiled.

"Where's the bride?"

"I think she is resting in her room."

"The bridegroom?"

"Oh, that one." Her mouth soured. "He has gone. He has been given his money and has gone."

To the right of the living room, as I faced the back of it, was the narrow kitchen. It appeared to be neat, well-scrubbed and well-kept. To the left rear of the room, level with the entrance to the kitchen, were large French doors. Earlier, when I'd asked directions to the bathroom, I was told to go through those French doors and follow the walk. The bathroom was at the back corner, beyond the kitchen, and it could only be reached from the yard. The bathroom, it turned out, was dark and foul and cold.

I couldn't see much of it but there appeared to be a large yard that was enclosed by a high wall. Against the wall, near it, I thought I could make out the leafless shapes of two or three small trees.

The vodka disappeared. We were on the third bottle. The Polish men were drinking it like they thought we'd take it away from them. I'd tried moving around the room, talking to the guests but mostly I got stone-eyed looks that didn't encourage me.

I just completed a tour of the room when I saw the bride for the first time. I heard Anna shout, "Here is my best friend," and turned and saw Anna with her arms open, about to rush across the room and embrace her. The girl was tall and slim, unlike the other Polish women at the party. Her hair was light, mussed now, and she wore a short white dress with a crushed bunch of blue flowers pinned to the right side of it.

Anna started for her and stopped. The bride was crying and gagging. I didn't understand the crying but I understood the gagging. The girl was one breath away from losing it all on the living room floor. Anna dropped her arms to her sides and groaned. The bride ran across the room, opened the French doors and ran outside.

"Mitka," Anna yelled after her. Then she followed and closed the doors behind her.

I'd opened a bottle of the Claret in the kitchen and dried the grease from what would have to pass as a wine glass. I entered the living room before I realized the music has stopped. I looked around. The three Polish women were gone, down the hallway to the bedrooms, I decided. The three Polish men were standing, one at the table and the other two with their backs against the wall behind him.

I reached the table. The man across it from me was dark haired and his face was pocked. There was a drunk sweat on his face even in the chill of the room. I was going to pour myself a glass of wine. I didn't. I placed the glass on the table and tamped the cork back into the wine bottle.

The man with the pocked face lifted the third of the vodka bottles. There was an inch or so left in it. He put the neck of the bottle to his mouth. I thought he was going to swallow. Instead, he lowered the bottle and spat the vodka onto the center of the table. "You will go now," he said.

I shook my head. "I don't think so. I'm having too much fun."

"You will go." It was the same flat tone of voice. I looked past him. The two men against the wall hadn't moved. A movement by the man with the pocked face drew my attention back to him. He'd reached into his trouser pocket. He brought out a knife. It wasn't a switchblade. It was a slide blade. A click and a push and the blade slid from the cover of the handle and locked in place. It wasn't a long blade but it looked sharp. "I will make you go."

I took a drag-leg step forward and moved the Claret bottle from my left hand into my right. He didn't switch the knife to his left hand to counter the move. A beginner, I thought. I flipped the wine bottle to my left hand and began a slow circle of the table toward him. He backed away, whipping the blade from side-to-side.

I needed an edge. It took me brief time to find one. His eyes followed the bottle of wine. I moved forward. I was at the end of the table, close enough, and I swung my right hand to the side and swept the table clean of empty vodka bottles, the sausage and crackers and the penny candy. One instant, that was what I needed. I got it. His eyes flicked to the left, toward the damage. I swung the wine bottle up, overhead, and down across the point of the man's right shoulder. He grunted and cursed and fell to one knee. The blade fell from his numbed fingers and rattled on the floor. I stepped forward and put a foot on the blade and pushed it aside. Almost with the same movement, I kicked the pocked man in the chest and knocked him into the chairs behind him.

There was screaming. The three women who'd gone down the hall had returned. They stood in the doorway yelling choruses of what I guessed was "bloody murder" in Polish. One of them, perhaps the pocked man's woman, was pulling her hair and crying.

I reached over and picked up the knife. I retracted the blade and dropped the knife in my pocket. The two men against the wall hadn't moved. In fact, they seemed pressed against the yellow plaster.

The French doors opened. Anna Piroski stood there. "Get out, get out." A torrent of Polish followed. "Leave. Leave now."

I turned and looked for my trench coat. I found it and placed the set-aside bottle of Claret on the table. I was putting on my coat when I realized Anna wasn't talking to me. She circled the table and stood beside me.

"Not you, Miami," she said,

The two men lifted the pocked man from the floor and held him upright. The three women collected their coats. After all the shouting and screaming, it was suddenly calm again. I didn't understand the words but I felt it in Anna's tone. She soothed them. She coaxed them. When they were at the doorway, Anna took a bottle of the Claret and pressed it upon them, insisting until they took it.

The door closed behind them. I was alone with Anna and the bride, wherever she was.

The bride, Mitka, was passed out in the bathroom. I stood outside and shivered while Anna cleaned her up the best she could. There was still a rank, vomit smell to the girl as I carried her into the house, through the living room and into her room at the end of the hallway.

The bed was mussed. There was a plaster cross on the wall over the bed. And I kicked an empty wine bottle as I leaned over the bed and placed Mitka on it.

I backed away, headed for the living room.

"Help me undress her," Anna said. "She is heavier than she looks to be."

I turned her this way and that while Anna removed her wedding dress. Then her white stockings and her shoes and the sheer half-slip. The girl's underwear was as sheer as the half-slip had been. I could see the cluster of curly pubic hair past the crotch of her underpants. The nipples of her small, almost perfect breasts were erect and hard.

I used the wine bottle as an excuse to back away. I picked it from the floor and placed it on the table beside the bed. When I turned, Anna was looking down at Mitka.

"Miami?"

"Yes."

"Would you rather make love to me or to Mitka?"

I cocked my finger and pointed it at Anna.

She laughed. "Now I will show you my room."

Before that was to happen, we straightened the living room. All the mess I'd made when I'd cleared the table. I found two glasses and poured from the bottle I'd opened and used as a club on the pocked man.

"To the bride," I said.

Anna drank. "Is this a good wine?"

"Fair," I said.

She smiled at me over the rim of the glass. "I was surprised, Miami. Many men, if they were given the choice between Mitka and me, would have taken Mitka."

I didn't say anything. I let her bounce the ball all she wanted. I sipped the wine.

"Do you have a woman in the States?"

Not anymore. Maybe I never really did.

"Two of them," I said.

"I thought you cared for me." Anna fluttered her eyes at me. "Now the truth is that you have two women."

"I'll send telegrams to Miami, Florida in the morning and tell both women that it is over between us."

"You would do that for me?"

"Sure, I would."

"You are a sweet man." Anna put a hand on my shoulder and ran the palm of it slowly down my arm.

I had the feeling I'd seen the movie before. Probably at some classic film festival and it had starred Greta Garbo. Before sound. With subtitles. The eye flutters, the touching, all belonged in that same film.

"Tell me about Harry Gault," I said.

She backed away, as if she'd been struck. Her eyes were down, hooded. When she lifted her eyes there was an incredible sadness on her face. "Now I know that you do not care for me. I should have allowed Lazlo and the others to hurt you."

"I appreciate you holding him back," I said.

"Lazlo is a very bad man with a knife."

That had to be some other Lazlo. This one was a pussycat. There were twelve-year old kids in Atlanta who could have carved their initials on Lazlo's forehead while he was deciding what he wanted to do with his knife.

I remembered that I had Lazlo's blade. I took it from my pocket and placed it on the table. "A man that bad with a knife ought to have his back."

Anna laughed. "Now you are making fun of me."

"Just a bit," I said. "Tell me about Harry Gault."

"He was my friend. One day he said he was going back to America. He said he was tired of England and the school."

"When was that?"

She closed her eyes, as if thinking. "It was in September."

"He didn't arrive in Atlanta."

"He spoke of New York several times." Anna opened her eyes. "I had the feeling he wanted to live in New York."

I gulped the Claret. "There is also the matter of the checks. The one you cash once-a-week and the other ones that pay the rent on this apartment and for other expenses."

"Harry said he did not need the money. He said he hated his grandfather's money." Anna placed her glass of wine on the table and found her purse next to my trench coat. "I will show you." She dug deep into the purse and brought up a book of checks. She opened it and held it toward me while she kept a tight grip on the end of it. She flipped the checks slowly so that I could see that each of them had been signed. "Do you see?"

I said I saw.

"Now, can I show you my room? I have wanted to show you my room since the time I met you in the Drug Store pub." She dropped the check book into her purse and closed it.

"Why did he sign all the checks?"

"He said he wanted to help me. He said he also wanted to help my friend, Mitka." A thoughtful, sad look crossed her face and then was gone. "In some ways, I think he liked Mitka better than he liked me."

It was a dead-end road. I decided I'd gone about as far as I could go. For now, anyway. I lifted my glass and tipped back what was left in it. "Yes, now you can show me your room."

Anna's body, after she undressed in the almost dark bedroom, reminded me of the "Standing Nude" by Gaston Lachaise that was in the courtyard of the Museum of Modern Art the last time I was there. But that was years ago.

I don't know if my body reminded her of anything.

I almost lost it. It almost got away. Just before she moved and pressed herself against me, she crossed herself.

I figured the time difference after I caught the cab. It was just after four a.m. London time. Five or six hour time difference made it ten or eleven back in Atlanta. I'd call Frank Butler at home.

Not much to say about Anna. In bed, she was lusty and she'd whimpered and cried at all the right times. But she'd been dry to me at first and I didn't take that as a compliment. I took it to mean that there was something going on in her mind and her body was on automatic pilot. We were both going through the motions and I wondered why either one of us bothered.

Before she slept, she'd said, "You are like a bull, Miami." That wasn't out of a Greta Garbe movie. It was probably a quote from some South American peasant movie classic.

I'd slept for an hour or so. Then I found my clothes and dressed in the living room. Before I left the apartment, I took the check book from Anna's purse and removed one of the signed checks from the back of it. That way she wouldn't miss it for a week or two.

At the hotel, I took a warm bath to take the chill away. I brushed my teeth to remove the last taste of the Polish vodka from my mouth, and called Frank Butler.

The call went straight through. From the clarity, I was fairly certain it had been placed on the satellite line. "I've got a big job for you," I said.

"Tell me about it."

First I'd told him about Anna and Mitka and what I'd learned about Harry. I told him I wanted all the flights from London to the States checked, from late August to the middle of September, to see if Harry was on any of them.

"You know how many flights there were during that period?" Frank asked.

"Sorry. But I've got to know if the girls are lying to me."

"And if they are?"

"Between us, if he didn't fly back to the States, I think the boy is dead." It was rougher than I meant it to be, but I was tired and feeling ragged.

The silence at his end of the line went on and on. I waited. It was his nickel and he could spend it any way he wanted to. "I'll rush it," Butler said. "And I hope you're wrong."

"How long?"

"A day. I'll call you."

I had a taxi drop me at the American Embassy. It was lunch time and Miles Carson was out until later in the day. His secretary, Donna, remembered me and I talked to her in the entrance-way, among the Marine guards, and gave her the signed check I'd taken from Anna Piroski's purse. I explained what I wanted. Mr. Carson, through whatever influence he had, through Scotland Yard or whoever, could authenticate the signature. There was probably a signature card at Barclay's on King's Road or there might be some documents Harry Gault had signed at the Embassy.

"I need it fast. Later this afternoon, if possible." I said I was expecting a call from Harrison Gault's lawyer that evening. If the answer was what I expected, then it was probably a police matter.

"This afternoon?" Donna seemed doubtful.

"Tell him I said pretty please. Pretty please with sugar on it."

From the look she gave me, I knew she hadn't been born in South Carolina or Georgia.

Miles Carson called me early in the evening. "You put me to a lot of trouble for nothing."

"How's that?"

"The signature is one hundred percent. It's the real article and I've got a statement from the Scotland Yard lab to prove it."

"The best lies are the ones with some truth in them."

"That doesn't make much sense," Carson said.

It did to me. "What time will you be at your desk in the morning?"

"Ten."

"I'll call you then."

I was asleep when the call came through. It was 2 a.m. London time. That was 8 or 9 p.m. Atlanta time. I never could quite figure it out.

"That was some job you gave me," Butler said. "I had to make the request through the F.B.I. Here's what I've got. I can't say this with one hundred percent certainty. What I can say is that all the airlines checked their computers, their passenger lists. Middle of August to the middle of September. Unless there was a slip-up, unless there's a mistake somewhere, Harry Gault didn't fly back to the States. He's still over there somewhere."

"Shit."

"What do we do now?" I could hear the anxiety in Frank Butler's voice.

"We see how helpful Scotland Yard is."

"When?"

"It's a bit after two here. Eight hours or so. I'll work through Miles Carson."

"The man at the Embassy?"

"Yeah."

"Has he been helpful?"

"You owe him a gold star so far."

Butler said he'd make sure the gold star went on Miles Carson's record.

"I hope I'm wrong about this."

"Find the truth. The old man can stand the truth, no matter what it is. It's the uncertainty that scares him."

I said I'd call as soon as I knew something. Before I fell asleep again, before my mind relaxed the claws that kept me awake, I wondered about the old man, about the myth that was Harrison Gault.

What kind of man would rather have the truth rather than a whisper of a dream?

Donna led me down the hallway. After we were safely beyond the Marine guards, she stopped and looked at me. "Mr. Carson is not happy with you this morning."

"That right?"

"After you called to make this appointment a telex arrived from Washington."

"What did it say?" I smiled.

"Do you think I read his messages?"

"Honey," I said, "I think you make his breakfast coffee and cook his eggs."

She blushed. I'll say that for her. "The telex said you were to be given whatever help you needed, to whatever lengths you wanted to go. Otherwise, Harrison Gault would fly over here and start breaking heads."

"In those exact words?"

She smiled. "I left out the obscene ones."

Donna left me at the door with a wave and what might have passed for a curtsy.

There was a brown tweed topcoat over the back of one of the chairs. I smelled it the moment I entered the room. It had the scent that most wool has in a season when there's rain about every other day. The man it belonged to sat across the desk from

Miles Carson, who introduced him as Inspector Dawson from Scotland Yard.

Dawson didn't look like any cop I'd ever met. He could have passed for the manager of one of the departments at Harrods. He was fair haired, athletic and he didn't look like he'd had his first shave yet.

Dawson was more than mildly irritated at me and the U.S. Embassy. "We don't usually make this kind of house call," he said.

"We appreciate the cooperation Scotland Yard is giving us," Carson said. His soft stroking would have had most people purring. Not Dawson. "I think you will understand that this is a tricky business."

"Perhaps you will be good enough to tell me what is tricky about it." Dawson bit into "tricky" like it was a sour apple.

Miles Carson spread it like he was going for a high yield on the corn crop this summer. When the verbal manure was about ankle deep, it was all I could do to keep from laughing.

Dawson heard as much as he wanted to. Then he sliced through it. "I do not see that we have sufficient cause to question these ladies."

I decided it was my turn. Low and fast might work where Carson's curves hadn't. "Maybe not, the way you see it. The way I see it we've got a missing boy. Let's put aside the fact that his grandfather can ring all the bells up to Buckingham Palace. Let's keep it simple. Just an American boy. He's not living where he's supposed to be and he's not living at the apartment where he's now paying rent. And we've then got that check book packed with checks that have already been signed. And we've got new money going into that account every month from his grandfather's account and we've got two Polish princesses living the good life on that money. Hell, for all I know, Harry Gault is living somewhere in Cornwall and trying to drink all the hard cider there. Or he's up in Scotland fishing for salmon. All we want to know, in the whole fucking world, is where the boy is. It's that simple. As far as I can see, the four days I've been here in London, the only people who can give me the answer I need are the two Polish girls. I talked to the one who wasn't passed out and I have reason to think she was lying to me."

"And you believe they might answer your question for me?"

"You're the law," I said.

"And if I am not willing to ask your question for you?" He'd asked the question of me but he was really talking to Miles Carson.

"The next request will come from our Ambassador." Carson looked at his watch. "In about one hour."

"And following that, the really heavy guns?" Dawson stood. He grabbed his tweed topcoat from the back of the chair. He started for the door and stopped and looked back at me. "Aren't you coming with me? I'll need a proper introduction to the princesses."

"Bloody politics." Dawson said that three or four times between almost clenched teeth before he calmed down. In his position I'd have felt the same way. I knew politics as well as he did. Maybe better. He could bitch but he had to do. Otherwise his hide got peeled and left out to dry.

It was handled smoothly. Dawson made the pickup at Dayville's while I waited in the car with his driver. The CLOSED FOR LUNCH appeared in the window glass of the door about two minutes after Dawson entered. From what he told me later, he allowed Anna to call her relief. He would arrive to open the shop within the hour.

When she reached the car, Anna stopped and looked at me. "Hello, Miami." Then she seated herself carefully next to me, so carefully that she did not touch me the whole drive to her apartment.

Over and over it. I sat on a chair in the corner of the living room and heard Anna's version of it. Partway through the third telling of it, Mitka arrived. One of Dawson's men had been dispatched to pick her up from a job she had at a coffee shop on Brompton Road. Mitka didn't seem to remember me from the wedding party.

Anna's version almost sang itself she told it so well.

Harry loved his grandfather but he had learned to hate his grandfather's money.

Before Harry left to return to the States, he'd signed all the remaining checks and told her that she and Mitka were to live on the money as long as it lasted. To Harry, it was some good coming of the evil way the money had been accumulated.

Harry was a nice boy and he loved both her and Mitka.

But he could not decide which of them he wanted to marry, so he had not married either of them. Instead, he had returned to America.

Dawson looked overcome by it all. Anna was back in the Greta Garbo role. Eyelids fluttering, the sighs, and the anguish. The pain of losing Harry. Mitka was her friend, her friend since they were children, but how jealous she had been when she knew Harry liked Mitka too.

I got to my feet and stretched and groaned.

Dawson, Anna and Mitka whirled and stared at me. I'd been rude by their standards. I'd interrupted their full concentration.

"The loo," I said. Less than a week in London and I was speaking the slang.

I opened the French doors and stepped into the yard. For the first time, I saw it in daylight. Sparse grass was browning, wintering. There was a stand of low hedges. A brick wall, about five feet high, enclosed the yard. There was a glint in the dull sun at the top of the wall. I walked in that direction. I was right. The enclosure was a throwback. Broken bottle glass was pressed into the mortar the length of the top rim. I turned and headed for the loo. I stopped and did an about-face. Three trees were in a row there, young trees, planted in the last two or three years. I didn't know what kind of trees they were. Fruit trees or ornamental, one or the other. The bare limbs I'd seen outlined against the sky on Wednesday night. The tree in the middle bothered me.

Hard to say why. A slightly different color. A stiffness. I took a couple of steps and reached the tree on the left. I put out a hand and broke a small twig from it. The twig gave, it had some bend to it. A pace to my right and I broke a twig from the tree in the center. It snapped, dry and brittle and dusty. Another step to my right and I broke a twig from the tree on my right. It gave to my touch. There was life in it.

I forgot my reason for going outside in the first place. The bathroom could wait. I returned to the house and opened the French doors and stood there until the cold air got Dawson's attention.

"What do you know about trees?" I asked Dawson.

CHAPTER FIVE

"Root damage," Dawson said. The center tree was on its side in the yard.

The digger, a man in blue coveralls, tossed his shovel onto the grass and stepped from the shallow hole. "It's here, the way the gentleman said it would be."

Anna stood in the open doorway with an arm around Mitka's shoulders. Mitka began to sob. She turned and buried her face in Anna's shoulder.

Anna stared at me. Her lips moved. Until that moment I didn't know that I could read lips. Anna said, *I should not have shown you my room, Miami.*

It was another emotional circus. Anna wanted to take all the blame. It appeared, for a time, that Mitka might let her. Then, so quickly I hardly saw the change, Mitka admitted that she and she alone had killed Harry Gault. For love, she said. She met Harry first and Harry seemed to love her. But he'd changed after he got to know Anna. Before Mitka knew what was happening, Anna was his favorite.

There was gypsy blood in her, Mitka admitted. At least her mother had said there was. Jealous and hurt, she plotted some way of getting revenge on Harry. One night, Harry got drunk and, to show off, he'd signed all the checks and said that money did not matter to him. Now, he said, she and Anna could buy anything they wanted. That same night, while Anna slept, Harry tried to get into her room. Mitka made him leave. Either that or she would make a scene that would awaken Anna.

The next morning Anna left for work early. Mitka's shift didn't start until noon. Harry was asleep in Anna's bed when Mitka dressed in her bathing suit and went into the yard to sunbathe on a blanket. She was there, half asleep, when Harry found her. "If he loved Anna more than he loved me, then why did he make advances to me in the yard that morning?"

"What kind of advances?" Dawson was taking notes.

"He forced me to make love to him. On the blanket beside the trees. He told me he would beat me if I told Anna. When he slept, I went into the kitchen and got the carving knife. I stabbed him in the heart." A fist thumped in the hollow between the small, hard breasts.

I sat in my chair in the corner and watched Anna. Anna chewed the knuckle of the thumb on her right hand. Her head moved, almost reflex shaking, as if she couldn't quite believe what she heard.

The rest of the dreary business. How she'd dug up the center tree, buried Harry under it, and replanted the tree. "I didn't know I would kill the tree," Mitka said. Then she was sobbing. Her face a ruin and a wasteland.

I thought I'd heard enough. It was break time in this lower-class tragedy. I got my coat. On the way to the door, I told Dawson I would be in town another day or two if he needed me. He said he would call if he did.

I reached the door and stopped. "When I returned from work that day," Anna said, "Mitka told me Harry had left for the States. I had no reason to believe she was lying."

I walked down the street to the main road and flagged a taxi.

I loafed around the hotel. I hadn't made the call to Butler in Atlanta yet. I told myself that I was letting him get his sleep. The truth was that I didn't want to make the call. I knew I'd have to, no matter how I felt. I had to be certain that Butler got to old man Gault before the news of his grandson's death did. Finally, I decided I'd waited long enough. I was about to place the call when the desk put through a call to me.

I recognized the spoon-bread accent that belonged to Miles Carson at the American Embassy. "Can you come over here right away?"

"I'd rather not. What's it about?"

"The Polish girl."

I thought he meant Mitka. My guess was that he wanted me to do through all I knew about the killing. "Look, why don't you talk to Dawson at the Yard? He's got it gift-wrapped by now."

"Not that girl," Miles said. "Anna Piroski."

"What about her?"

"Get your butt over here. This has got my mind boggled."

"I stashed Anna in an office down the hall with Donna," Carson said.

The paper he passed across the desk to me was partly in Polish and partly in English. I could understand enough of it and guess the rest. It was a record of a marriage between Harry Gault, III and Anna Piroski at the Free Polish Church of London. It had been performed on August 8th at 5 p.m. by Father S.J. Vozzek.

I read it slowly, what I could, and returned the document to Carson. "You believe this?"

"I've got to." Carson placed the marriage record on his desk and passed a photo to me. It was a picture of Anna and the boy, Harry, in front of the church. It looked more like a storefront than a church. A man in a priest's outfit stood behind them. "I sent a runner to talk to Father Vozzek. It's true enough. He remembers the boy."

"Why?"

"Why what?"

There were a lot of whys. I gave him my first one. "Why did he marry her?"

"Love," Miles Carson said. "Or the sex itch."

The sex itch wasn't that hard to scratch. Or was I being too hard on Anna? There was a certain quality about her that didn't fit any of the usual molds. "The second why. Why didn't Anna tell us about the marriage before this?"

"It bothered me too," Miles said. "Anna says Harry wanted the marriage kept secret. When he left or disappeared, she was hurt. She believed that Harry had wanted the marriage kept secret so that he could abandon her when the time came. That he had married her in bad faith. And, along with that, she kept her secret because she didn't want to hurt Mitka. According to her, if Mitka knew that she had lost all hope, Mitka might have killed herself."

"You believe her?"

Miles shrugged his shoulders. "What I think doesn't really matter. You're here because I thought you'd want to pass the word to Atlanta."

"All right." I got my trench coat from the coat rack.

"That's not all the news."

"Huh?"

"Anna says she's pregnant," Miles said.

"By Harry Gault?"

"Who else?"

I closed my eyes and shook my head. All I did was stir around the darkness in there. "I'd better go back to the hotel and make the call. It's in Frank Butler's hands now. You'll hear from him."

"I thought I might."

Halfway across the world, I thought I could hear the gears meshing in Frank Butler's mind. First the bad news, sir. Your grandson, Harry, is dead. Now the good news. Before his death, he married a foreign girl.

A white girl, Mr. Butler?

Oh, yes, sir. The rest of the good news is that Harry's widow is in a family way. That's right. This could be your great grandchild. Perhaps even a son. Your great grandson.

"When are you flying back, Jim?"

"Soon as I can get a flight."

"Stay another day or two. Enjoy yourself. There's a chance Mr. Gault will want you to escort the girl here."

I didn't have to think about that. "I'd rather not."

"It could be that your druthers don't have anything to do with it." Frank Butler could be a hard, realistic man when he had to be.

When the American government wanted to, they could roll rocks uphill. By the first of the week it was all but completely arranged.

I stayed away from Anna. She called a couple of times. Frank Butler had arranged that she move from the flat and into a suite at the Dorchester, one of the nicest hotels in Europe. I got that much and the room number. But I wasn't taking calls, and I wasn't in my hotel room any more than I had to be, and I didn't answer the messages that got stuffed in my pigeon hole at the desk.

I was in a rank temper. I was being treated as hired help. It's what I was, but I didn't have to like it.

I got word on Monday that the flight had been arranged from the Atlanta end. It would be a Tuesday flight into Hartsfield International. I dug one of the notes from the pile that had collected on my dresser top and called the Dorchester. I gave the suite number.

Anna answered. I knew her voice. "This Mrs. Gault?"

She said it was. I told her the flight plans. I'd pick her up by taxi at ten the next morning. She wasn't to worry about luggage. If her bags were over the weight, we would pay the excess. Those were my orders from Atlanta. "You have plenty of cash for all your needs?"

"Mr. Gault has been kind," Anna said.

I said I understood.

"I have found a solicitor for Mitka," Anna said.

I said that was kind of her.

"Mitka is still my friend, no matter what she did."

I grunted. I was running out of nice, polite words.

"I am having a few friends here tonight. I wonder if you would like to come. It is a goodbye party."

"Your Polish army? No thanks. I'm busy."

"I understand," Anna said.

"You understand what?"

"That you hate me, Miami."

I let that hang in the wind for a time. Then I said I would be at the Dorchester at ten the next morning. "Please be ready."

Anna said that she would.

Anna waited in the lobby for me. One suitcase and one overnight bag at her feet. When she stood, I realized that she'd spent at least part of one day in a clothing store. She wore a gray dress that pointed to all the right places. Her high heeled shoes looked like they'd probably gone for about a hundred and fifty pounds. I helped her with a wool coat that had a real fur collar. She clutched a matching purse and gloves.

The taxi driver placed her bags in the trunk next to mine. I sat next to Anna and watched her open her coat so that I could admire her dress.

"Do you think I look nice?"

I said she did.

"Like a real American?"

"Better," I said. "More European."

She laughed. Pleased with herself, I thought.

I drank and slept. Drank and slept. Frank Butler had thought of everything. He'd booked us into first class and he'd even reserved us a table in the small dining room above the first-class cabin. It seated only twelve. She carried herself as if she'd been born to the life of a princess.

There was Beluga and Russian vodka and after that poached fresh salmon and good French wines. I could see the other men, in the cabin below and in the dining room, the way they looked at her. Perhaps she looked older than her twenty-one years. Maybe it was the wedding ring she wore. The expensive clothes. There was a scent of money about her and everybody smelled it. Maybe it wasn't the best taste, the way she spent it, but there was money. Many things can be forgiven if there is money.

After we returned from the dining room, the attendant cleared the small reading area in the front of the cabin. A movie screen was lowered. I ordered a Calvados and a black coffee to finish off lunch. Beside me Anna unwrapped the earphones and adjusted them so they didn't spoil her hairdo.

I sipped the Calvados and thought of twisted apples, hard as stone to the core.

I missed the main titles and I wasn't sure what the movie was. I'd refused the earphones. Without the sound it didn't make much sense to me. There were fast, fancy cars and beautiful women and one hot tub scene. I watched Anna, the child with all her new toys.

After ten minutes, Anna removed the earphones and turned slightly in her seat so that she faced me. I'd finished the last of the

Calvados. I'd passed the glass to the stewardess and she brought me another.

"You drink too much," Anna said. There was a serious, critical look on her face.

"You an expert on drinking?"

"I am Polish."

"I guess that does qualify you," I said.

She took the glass from my hand and sipped the Calvados. She sighed. "It is good."

I nodded.

"I will have one also."

I ordered for her.

"When we reach Atlanta, will we be good friends?" Anna asked.

"I don't think so."

The stewardess brought Anna the Calvados and a cup of coffee. Anna returned the coffee to her.

"Why not, Miami?"

"We'll be in different worlds there," I said. "I don't get invited often to the Gault Farm."

"Or at all? Is that what you are saying?"

"Close," I said.

Anna took a huge swallow of Calvados and swished it around in her mouth before she swallowed. "I think I will insist."

"Huh?"

"I will insist we be friends."

With the time difference it was late afternoon when we arrived in Atlanta, I collected our baggage and we worked our way through customs. I paid a small tax on three extra bottles of a single malt scotch I'd brought back as a gifts. And then we were past customs and I saw Frank Butler and the driver. The driver wore a dark suit and carried a cap in his hands. Frank allowed me to introduce him to Anna. He was old south courtly to her and bowed over her hand. The driver took her bags and Frank took one of mine. We rode one of the shuttle cars from the concourse into the main terminal.

Frank Butler and I stood across the car from Anna and the driver. "As you can imagine," Frank said, "the old man is upset about his grandson."

I nodded.

"Still, he thinks you did a good job under the circumstances. Miles Carson was good enough to fill us in on your part in the matter." His eyes measured me. "There was no reason to hide your light under a basket."

"I always wanted to be Perry Mason."

His head angled toward Anna. "What about the girl?"

"I think she'll be good for Gault. In a lot of ways, she's like a child. That's what's keeping him alive, I think. The possibility there will be a great grandchild. If it hadn't been for that, I think the shock would have killed him."

There wasn't much to say. I waited.

"He has authorized a bonus for you."

"Thank him for me."

"You'll come by my office in the morning?"

I nodded. "Let me call you in the morning and set a time. I'm worn out."

When we reached the terminal, Anna wanted to give me a ride into town. Frank explained to her that they were not going in that direction. So, we said our polite goodbye.

I took a taxi into town.

It was bitchy cold in Atlanta. It made London seem warm. I unpacked my things and slept for three hours. Then I dressed and drove to George's Deli and entered through the back door. The juke box was playing an old Willie Nelson record that was scratchy and almost needled through. The record remained on the box because I said I'd take my business somewhere else if they ever removed it. *The Sound In My Mind* played while I stood at the end of the bar and waited for Sam Najjar to notice me and bring me a bottle of Bud.

I said, "I know you don't drink this shit," and passed him one of the bottles of single malt scotch.

Midnight. The phone was ringing when I unlocked the door and entered the house. I answered it.

Anna didn't have to tell me her name. "When will you show me your room?"

"Not this year," I said. I listened to her breathing for a few seconds and then I broke the connection and left the phone off the hook so I could sleep.

CHAPTER SIX

The funeral for Harrison Gault, III was an outrageous affair. The mourners were restricted to family and close friends only, according to the papers, and the burial took place at the old family plot there on the Gault Farm. The news media wasn't allowed through the gates. The Governor dispatched enough Highway Patrolmen to control a drunk crowd at a University of Georgia football game, with orders that no one was to crash the funeral.

A television helicopter from an Atlanta station hovered a distance away, beyond the property boundary, while a prayer service was held inside the main house. About the time the casket was carried to the graveside, two armed Air National Guard helicopters appeared and flanked the news helicopter. The pilot and cameraman were escorted to a nearby landing field where the two men were detained until the brief ceremony ended.

"Highhanded" was what the General Manager of the Atlanta station called it.

"An invasion, for commercial purposes, of a sacred privacy," Frank Butler, on behalf of the Gault family, thundered back.

I wasn't at the funeral. I wasn't invited and didn't expect to be.

The day after I arrived back from London, I called Frank Butler and begged off the planned meeting. A couple of days later, I mailed him an accounting of my expenses. There was two or three hundred left from the expense money advanced me. Butler subtracted that from the $1,390 he figured he owed me for the one week and the part of the second week. Another thousand was thrown in, the bonus old Gault wanted me to have.

That winter, the trial in London was big news in the Atlanta papers. The trial didn't last long. Rumor, I heard, had it that the old man had sent one of Butler's best young men to London to work on the sidelines with the lawyers hired to defend Mitka. There were mitigating circumstances, I suppose, and she pled guilty to the murder of Harry Gault. There was little or no mention of Anna's position in the triangle.

Mitka received a ten-year sentence and began serving it at the Wickwire Detention Center for Women.

Time passed. Winter thawed. Spring came at last.

In late May, the newspapers were full of it: an heir to the Gault fortune had been born. A boy. What the old man wanted. And what the old man wanted, he usually got. Another Harrison Gault. A happy ending to a sad business. Wasn't that the way it was supposed to be in the best of all possible worlds?

I saw Anna again for the first time that summer.

It was August. I was in the lounge of the Peachtree Plaza Hotel, where the green water of the artificial lake runs through it. It wasn't enough to serve watered-down, over-priced booze anymore. You needed a water feature, too. But Hump and I weren't there for the booze or the architecture. We were there for the trim. Office trim, uptight business women in need of a good loosening.

I wasn't very good at the pick-up game, so I'd let Hump do all the work and I'd get his cast-offs. Hump managed to catch the eye of two office girls, secretaries or stenographers, who were drinking white wine at a table near us. After a time, they joined our table.

During a pause in the conversation, I looked over my shoulder toward the staircase. I blinked and looked again. The woman on the stairs was Anna. The same dark hair but the fair skin was tanned now. She wore a white dress that made the tan seem even darker.

I said, "Excuse me for a second," and left the table. I got two steps before I stopped. A man in a gray silk blend suit appeared on the step just behind Anna and placed a hand on her elbow. She turned to him and laughed. His hand moved from her elbow and touched her waist with a kind of possession I understood. I lowered my head and returned to my table. Hump looked up from his drink. There was a question on his face.

"Thought I saw somebody I knew," I said.

We went back to the empty small talk with the girls. At the right moment, as if I'd timed it, I turned in my chair, Anna's back was to me and she was walking toward the arcade that led to Peachtree Street. The man in the gray silk blend suit hesitated long enough to light a cigarette. I took a mental photograph of him. He was about my height, six feet or so, with almost blue-black hair. There was a feathering of premature gray around the sides. His face was in hard angles and he had dark eyes and dark eyebrows.

After he lowered his gold lighter, he puffed to be certain the cigarette was lit and then he resumed a graceful, quick walk that brought him level with Anna in no time at all.

The face was familiar. It itched at me. I'd seen it somewhere.

The office girl said her name was Veronica. She was young and firm fleshed. I was neither. We grunted and rolled around in my bed for a time until I was tired enough to sleep. I could have got the same result from jogging a couple of miles, though that probably would have killed me. But I said she was great and she said I was, too, the polite lies we tell just to get by. I put her in a cab and I went back to bed. The sheets smelled too much of her, of perfume and lotions and talc. And faintly, it seemed, of scorched hair. I stripped the bed and lay on the bare mattress.

I stared at the ceiling. The face of the man who'd been with Anna at the Plaza cooked in my mind's eye. *Somewhere. Somewhere. Something to do with trucking.*

Then it came to me.

He was Carl Busco. Almost mob, but not quite. But that was only because Atlanta, the last time I'd heard, was considered an open city, not controlled by just one family. The city was fair game for anybody who wanted to try and operate here. Busco was down from Jersey, hired by Amalgamated Trucking, an association of eight trucking firms, to help break a strike with the Teamsters. Busco, billing himself as a Labor Relations Consultant, did it by paying off the Teamster leaders. Strike over. Drivers shafted.

That Carl Busco.

I was having coffee and trying the crossword puzzle on Monday morning when Frank Butler called. "How do you like this weather, Jim?"

I said that it was fine if you never had to walk around in it.

Small talk was over. "Jim, can you come by my office for a few minutes? I need the benefit of your devious thinking."

"Hold a minute." I thought about whether I wanted to get caught up in another rich man's domestic mess. The truth was I was bored. "I can make it."

"Ten minutes?"

I said I'd be there.

❧   ❧   ❧

Butler's secretary poured good coffee. She looked like Miss America without a girdle. I watched her soft, puckered rump as she left the office and closed the door behind her.

"What's this about?" I asked him. "When did you ever run into anything you weren't devious enough to handle yourself?"

He shook his head. "Anna Gault."

"You handle her and I'll handle your secretary."

"Jim, I'm serious."

I wasn't bored anymore. But a chill wind blew across my shoulder blades. "What now?"

He opened a desk drawer on his right. He placed a dark velvet cloth on his desk. Slowly, carefully, he opened the folds of the cloth. Whatever it was glittered at me.

"You mind?" I asked. He shook his head. I picked it up and straightened it over the palm of one hand. It was a necklace, a small one, the kind I think they called a choker. It held five matched emeralds in a row, each stone surrounded by clusters of diamonds. "These real?"

"Real," he said. "As real as the owner, Anna Gault."

I didn't know much about the value of emeralds. What I'd heard was that stones larger than a carat were rare and especially valuable. Each gem was the size of the nail on my little fingers. With the value of the diamonds, the choker was big money. "Stolen?"

"No."

"Hocked?"

"Sold. Outright sold. Bill of sale and all." The way Butler told it, the police were hassling a small-time gem dealer. An informant said he was fencing hot stones. A bust uncovered a cache of stolen gems, stones that had been taken from their mountings. A number of the gems were identified by a new method of x-raying the stones the insurance companies used. So, the police had the dealer cold. He was facing time. In the stash, but not on any of the stolen lists, was the necklace I was holding. The dealer denied the necklace was stolen and be produced a bill of sale to prove it. The policeman in charge of the investigation recognized the Gault name. He asked around and was told that Butler's law firm handled all the Gault affairs. He'd come to Frank. Was the bill of sale authentic?

"Was it?" I weighed the necklace in my hand. I'd never held anything so valuable before in my life and probably never would again.

"That's the delicate question," Butler said. "You see, I recognized the necklace immediately. I was there when Harrison Gault presented it to Anna. It was a mark of affection, a gesture, after little Harry was born."

"So you can't go to old Gault?"

"Never."

"Ask Anna."

"I did. She said it was none of my business."

I placed the necklace on the velvet cloth. I got out a pack of Pall Malls and lit one. Butler pushed a crystal ashtray toward me. "You got the bill of sale?"

He passed it to me. It looked neat and legal. For a sum of twenty-five thousand, Anna Gault had sold the necklace to Frederick Westcott. The necklace was described in detail in the bill of sale. After I finished with it, I passed it across the desk to Butler. "Twenty-five thousand?"

"That's hardly a fifth of what it is really worth. I had a look at the insurance papers. It is listed there for a hundred and ten thousand. That was four years or so ago. I had a dealer appraise it at a somewhat higher value, close to a hundred and fifty thousand."

I puffed at the cigarette. "Well, it's Anna's and I guess she can do with it what she wants to."

"Nothing is that simple," Butler said. "You've heard of the part of the Senate term Harrison spent in Washington? While he was there, he did a favor for one of those South American strongmen, one or other of the dictators. I think Harrison got him aid money or arms add or got his son accepted at Harvard. That Christmas, the South American presented Mrs. Gault with the necklace. The rest of her life, Mrs. Gault loved this necklace. Until now, until it turned up in the hands of a shady dealer, it was on the way toward becoming a family heirloom."

I was getting impatient. "All right, say all this is true..."

"I need to know what the hell is going on with Anna. Old Gault gives her all the spending money she wants. Hell, she receives an allowance that is probably more than you make in a year."

"Probably five years. Tell me about devious."

"I need a certain kind of man and you know her."

I waved that pitch aside. "That's the problem."

"You've got the street connections. I have to know why a rich widow needs twenty-five thousand dollars in hand. A day or two. That's all I'm asking."

"You remember Hump Evans?" I asked. Butler nodded. Hump had worked with me on the Chambers thing. "I can put him on this and give him directions. She's never seen him and he's got better street connections than I do. That's as far as I'll go."

Butler hesitated. I thought he might turn it down. Finally, he looked at me and nodded.

I mashed the cigarette butt in the crystal ashtray. I stood, "What about the necklace?"

"What?"

"The necklace."

"Mr. Westcott was kind enough to sell it back to the Gaults. I convinced him he needed the money more than he needed the questions that possession might raise about it."

I started for the door. "I saw Anna the other night."

"Where?"

"The Peachtree Plaza Hotel."

"What did she say?"

"She didn't see me." I reached the door and stopped with a hand on the doorknob. "You know a man named Carl Busco?"

A shake of his head. "Should I?"

"She was with him."

"Who is Busco?"

"That's a question around Atlanta. One version is that he's a hood. That he has mob ties."

"Anna keeps rough company"

"That's the way it seems."

On the way to the street, in the elevator. I roughed myself a kick or two for letting Butler involve me another time. All I could find on the good side of the ledger was that Hump probably needed the money. On the bad side, the part I didn't like to admit, I knew that Anna was on me like beggar's lice and I wanted the answers as much for myself as I wanted them for Frank Butler.

Hump said, "Bourbon with a beer chaser."

We were in a slum bar on Ponce De Leon. In the evening, the bar had wet t-shirt nights and go-go dancers who hid their hysterectomy scars under stick makeup and powder. In the late afternoon, as it was now at five, there were a few street crazies and winos spaced about the place. The bar was dark and over-heated and it smelled of last year's beer and the defeated sweat on the winos. It was still a nicer place to drink than the Peachtree Plaza Hotel.

I drank two beers. He let me treat him to two bourbons and a single chaser.

"It's pretty fucking vague," Hump said.

"I'm telling you how it got handed to me."

"Where do I start?"

"You know the Gault Farm in ..." I stopped. A guess floated past me and I grabbed it. "Give me a minute." I carried change to the pay booth in the back corner of the bar. I found the number, repeated it to myself a couple of times and dialed The Peachtree Plaza Hotel.

Yes, there was a Mrs. Harrison Gault registered. Did I want the number rung? I said I did. I let the phone ring twice and broke the connection before anyone could answer.

I returned to the table. "Start at the Peachtree Plaza Hotel."

"She lives there?"

"Visiting, I think."

"The pay?" he said.

"Hundred a day and reasonable expenses." I got my roll from my pocket and counted five twenties and slid them across the table toward him.

"Thanks."

"One thing," I said. "When I saw her the other night, she was with a guy named Carl Busco. The name mean anything to you?"

"No."

"Go to the library, look up the newspapers from the time of the trucking strike. He was brought in by Amalgamated Trucking for labor relations. I think he was in a picture or two."

"He come in to break heads?"

"Mostly to spread money around, buy off the union leadership. What I'm saying is that you ought to know what he looks like. If he's with her, and you're tailing him, he might think he's the one interests you and he might not like it."

"Got you." Hump poured down the rest of his chaser and stood.

"Take care."

"Always do."

He left through the back door. I sat over the bottom of the second beer. As soon as he was gone, I had a bad feeling, a chill in the heated bar room. He really hadn't been listening to me when I tried to warn him. He could be too self-confident. That was a risk when you were six-six with muscles like rebar.

It was after one in the morning by the bedside clock when I heard the doorbell. It rang for several long bursts while I found my slippers and stepped into an old pair of trousers, Before I reached the living room whoever it was had given up on the bell and was pounding on the door with his fist.

I opened the door. Hump leaned against the door frame. There was a white bandage patch on his forehead and his bottom lip was swollen. "What the hell, Hump?"

"I need a drink."

I motioned him inside and led the way to the kitchen. I switched on the overhead light. Now that he was in strong light, I saw the bristle of stitches on his lower lip. Five or six was my guess. I found the bottle of bourbon and poured him a huge shot in a juice glass. "You want a chaser?"

"Not this time." He poured back half the drink and winced when the alcohol touched the raw spot in his mouth. "At first, I thought about coming over here and bleeding on your floor."

"Bleed on it all you want. The maid comes in tomorrow." I was joking to cover my own guilt. I should never have let him follow Anna alone. I should have had his back the way he always had mine. "Sit down, Hump."

I got myself a glass and dropped in a couple of ice cubes. Now that I was awake, I knew I'd better have a drink with him or I wouldn't sleep after he left. I poured bourbon over the ice and rattled the drink in my hand.

"My better thought was to go by Georgia Baptist and have them ship the bill for the repairs to you."

ALL KINDS OF UGLY

"All right. That's an expense."

"That Busco is a sweetheart."

"I tried to tell you that." I sipped the bourbon and felt it burn my stomach.

"I didn't think he'd tumble to me so fast."

I poured him another shot and he told me his story.

After Hump left me at the bar, he'd called The Man, the black Godfather of Atlanta, for the word on Busco. We'd done some odd jobs and favors for The Man over the years. Hump more than me.

The Man knew all about Busco. Started out shylocking on the docks in New Jersey and then moved on to drugs. Heat on him in New York moved him south. Or maybe he was sent by one of the families to stake a claim. After Busco's work for Amalgamated Trucking, he'd opened a consulting firm with a suite of offices on West Peachtree.

"What kind of consulting?" I asked.

"Investments," Hump said. "Packaging."

"Huh?"

"Putting the borrowers together with the lenders. A way of cleaning dirty money."

"The Man told you all that?"

Hump nodded. "He's been keeping an eye on Busco."

Hump went on with his story. He couldn't find a photo of Busco in the newspapers so settled for a description from The Man. And he knew Busco's age. That much would have to do.

He drove to the Plaza and parked in the underground garage. A security man he knew at the hotel ran a check for him. Yes, Mrs. Gault was in her room. Hump got himself a drink and positioned himself so that he could watch the elevators and the desk. A few minutes after eight, a man stepped from the elevator. On the same elevator, there was a couple and a bellhop and a baggage cart so Hump guessed he'd come from the garage. The man fitted the description of Busco. The man used one of the house phones to make a call. Five or six minutes later, he was joined by a large dark-haired woman who matched the description I had given him of Mrs. Gault.

He followed them to the street. Across the street and to Peachtree Center and down the stairs to the Midnight Sun. They entered the restaurant. He entered the bar and found a seat that allowed him to watch the restaurant through a doorway. An hour and a half passed. Busco and Mrs. Gault left the Midnight Sun. Hump followed them back to the Plaza. They didn't enter the hotel. They walked around the side and entered the garage from the street level. Hump was close enough to see them drive away in a black Lincoln. He was a block behind them. The tail led him into northeast Atlanta. To Briarcliff and to a new condominium there. He parked four cars down from the Lincoln and waited. He wasn't sure exactly what he is waiting for. He saw a light go on in the condominium that Busco and the lady entered.

He was still there twenty minutes later, stamping his feet and trying to stay warm, when a blue Impala pulled into the parking lot right behind him so that he couldn't back out.

"And then?" I rolled the last of my drink down my throat.

"Two men invited me in for a talk."

"And you went?"

"I didn't see a lot of choice. One of them had iron. I wasn't carrying."

Carl Busco was waiting for Hump in the living room. There was no sign of the lady the whole time he was there. Maybe she was off in some other part of the apartment. Anyway, they wanted some answers to some questions. Busco wanted to know why Hump was tailing him.

"Not you," Hump said. "Mrs. Gault."

"Why?" Busco popped a knuckle and stared at him.

Hump told them that he'd been hired to follow the lady around for a few days.

"Who hired you?"

Hump told them that information was confidential. That was the wrong answer. It got him a skin tear on his forehead, fifteen stitches, the result of being slapped by the barrel of a .357.

He told them.

"Who'd you name?" I pulled the bourbon toward me and poured a trickle over the ice.

"You. I could've thrown the lawyer, Butler, into the pot. But he can't take care of himself. You can."

I nodded. "And then what happened?"

"Busco says for me to find myself another job."

The bourbon soured on my tongue, like a wine that had turned the corner and was headed for the vinegar carafe.

"Busco wears this pinkie ring on the little finger of his right hand. He makes a point of how much he wants me to find other work by backhanding me to the mouth." Hump touched his lip. "That's when I got this."

Busco nodded at the two men. He was done with Hump. The two men walked him outside and to his car. The parking lot was empty in all directions. One of the two men worked Hump over. Chest, stomach and ribs. Hump couldn't fight back because the other man held a gun to his head, otherwise he could've taken them both without breaking a sweat. That knowledge probably hurt Hump more than the beating.

The two men threw Hump into his car, closed the door and drove away. It took maybe twenty minutes for Hump to pull himself together enough to drive to Georgia Baptist for the patch-up.

"The doctor bill might run fifty." Hump said.

"I'll see that it's covered."

"Busco and his muscle know me now. I'm burned."

"You want to stay here tonight?"

Hump shook his head. "Sleeping on that couch would hurt me more than my beating."

"I'd give you the bed."

"That lumpy shit? No thanks."

I helped him to his feet and followed him to the door. "I'm sorry about this."

He stopped in the doorway and rubbed his ribs. "You know you're next in line. I had to give you to them. You mad, Jim?"

I shook my head. "I'm glad you did. It got you out alive and in one piece."

I watched him drive away. He might have been the only true friend I had and I'd nearly gotten him killed. And for what? I returned to the house and had another drink in the kitchen. I slept that night with my .38 Police Positive on the table beside my bed.

I rolled from bed the next morning late. After I brushed the sleep from my tongue, I put the gun in my coat pocket and drove downtown to Wilma's Cafe. Wilma's is a breakfast and lunch place. Usually full of lawyers and office workers. The cafe serves good sausage biscuits and coffee so rank it can scour the night ashes from a man's mouth.

I was a couple of doors away from Wilma's when I heard my name called. I heard the sound of boots behind me. I turned and reached into my pocket for my .38 Police Positive. I took my hand off the gun when I saw Anna trotting across the street toward me. She was dressed in designer jeans, a red blouse and soft black boots. Her hair was cut shorter than I remembered it. The tan still bothered me. I remembered when her skin was fair and pale.

"Yeah?" I waited for her. I knew how I looked. Unfriendly and distant.

At the curb, close to me, she tripped and I reached out a hand and caught her arm and steadied her. "I know the year is not completed, Miami, but I ..."

"A year was a rough estimate anyway." My hand remained on her elbow. I turned her and guided her toward Wilma's. "How about coffee and a sausage biscuit?"

When I returned to the side table after a trip through the serving line, she was smoking a cigarette and staring out the window. I placed a coffee in front of her and watched her add sugar and cream. I pushed a sausage biscuit across the table, near her coffee cup.

"How do I eat it?"

"Any way you want to." I fixed mine. A glob of catsup, some black pepper and a few drops of Texas Pete hot sauce. I took a bite and chewed and swallowed. "You were there last night, weren't you, when my friend got his beating."

"I was ... how you say ... passed out."

"You're up early today." I sipped the coffee and felt the heat of the coffee rub against the heat from the Texas Pete.

Anna lifted the sausage biscuit. She took a tiny bite from one side of it and made a face. She placed the biscuit on the dish and pushed it toward me. "Could I have toast instead?"

When I returned with the order of toast, I saw that my coat hung differently on the back of my chair. She'd checked to see what I was reaching for in my pocket. I put the toast in front of her and sat down. I watched as she buttered a toast wedge and added jelly. "This is much better."

"Anything you want," I said. "When I invite somebody to breakfast…"

"I realize you didn't invite me." One of Wilma's girls passed the table and stopped long enough to heat our coffee with a partial refill. Anna waited until the girl moved away before she lifted a hand and touched the zipper case. "Sometimes I think about what happened in London. Perhaps you *are* as bad as Lazlo."

It took me a few seconds to remember Lazlo. The Pole with the knife. "He was a beginner."

Her eyes cut toward my coat pocket. "If you carry that…"

"In the best of all worlds, if Busco gets to carry a piece, everybody else gets to carry two."

"You are angry because I was there with him?"

It was a woman's logic. I was jealous. I had her followed so that I could discover who it was she was seeing. Why not satisfy her? "A little. It bothered me a little."

"Only a little?" She flirted with me.

I insisted it was only a little.

"All you have to do if you wish to see me is call me."

"You're never home when I call." I finished my sausage biscuit and placed what was left of hers on my plate. I added catsup and black pepper. I was still trying for the perfect way to doctor a sausage biscuit.

"Carl is not happy with you."

"Fuck him."

"He wants you to leave him alone."

"Fuck what he wants."

"Oh, you." She stood and pushed her chair away from the table. The chair back banged against the well. I had a look into hard and angry eyes before she whirled and ran for the door.

The length of Wilma's people stopped talking and watched the scene. I chewed another bite from the sausage biscuit and stared back at them, eye-to-eye. Half-a-minute after the door closed behind Anna, the talk resumed and the tension eased.

I stared down at my coffee. I wasn't sure how much time passed before I smelled her perfume again and I heard the soft tap of her boot heels. "I don't want you for an enemy. You would be a terrible and frightening enemy." She moved the chair closer to the table and sat down again.

"I'm not your enemy."

"You are not as you were in London."

"That was a job," I said.

"No, it was more than a job. You truly liked me there in London. I liked you, too. But I hated you the day they found Harry's body. I was sure I'd never want you to touch me again."

Wilma's girl passed the table again. I pointed down at the cups. We'd had the one free refill. She hesitated until I passed her a dollar hill. She poured and shoved the dollar in her apron pocket.

"When I got here it was a strange country," Anna continued. "I did not know anyone. I knew that as soon as I reached Mr. Gault's farm. The only person I thought I knew was you. But when I called you that night..."

"I didn't think old Mr. Gault would want you hanging about with the hired help."

"I asked him about you." Her gray eyes regarded me evenly, stubbornly.

"He said you were good at what you did but that what you did was not very honest."

"That's me."

"Still, you were honest enough for him to send you to do his work in London."

"Available," I said. "I was available."

"But he trusted you to do his work honestly."

"From what I've heard of old Gault, I'd place a bet he and Frank Butler looked at it from every angle. They labored over it until they were sure there was no way I could gain an advantage over them. That there was no way I could profit from a dishonest urge if one happened to come on me."

"I am sorry for you, Jim."

"What for?"

"You have a broken back. Like a cat that has been run over in the road. You crawl and creep and slide on your stomach."

I looked at Anna. She chewed at the final wedge of cold toast. "One day I'll tell you which truck ran over me," I said.

"It would please me to know."

I lit a Pall Mall and waved a hand to push the smoke away from her. "Carl Busco send you?"

A hesitation while she blinked at my stare. "Yes, he did."

"The message?"

"He wants you to stay away from him."

"And from you, Anna?"

"Yes."

"I'll make a deal with you. You do a favor for me, and I'll back away from Busco."

"Very well."

"I want you to talk to Frank Butler. I'll call him now and see when he can meet with you."

"I have already talked to him. Why should I have to be questioned by him again?"

"He wants the truth about the necklace, Anna."

"The necklace was mine to do with as I pleased."

"I think you missed something. That necklace is on the way toward being a family heirloom. Someday, when your son is grown and he marries, you might want to pass that necklace down to his wife."

"Is that what's expected of me?"

"It's an old southern custom," I said.

"I do not understand Americans."

I wasn't done with her. "And it is another old southern custom not to be ripped off when you sell something. That necklace has been insured for over a hundred thousand dollars. It's been appraised in the last day or two for even more than the insured value."

"I didn't know."

"I didn't think you did."

"Twenty-five thousand seemed such a huge sum of money. More money than I could imagine anything could be worth."

"Now you know."

"I will see your Mr. Butler."

"Good girl." I used the phone in the other corner of the cafe to call Butler. I dialed his private number, the one that didn't go through the office switchboard.

"How bad is your man hurt?" Butler asked.

"Bruises and stitches. I said we'd take care of his medical."

"We will."

"I've talked to Anna. Can you see her now, this morning?"

"It's a bit after ten now. I can see her at ten-thirty."

"I'll point her in your direction," I said.

"You coming with her, Jim?"

"Nope. I've got work to do."

"Put in a voucher for the job."

"You've heard it. Two hundred for Hump and his medical expenses when I get the bill."

"Nothing for yourself?"

"I didn't do anything."

"You're making it hard for me."

"That's how I planned it. You keep trying to involve me in your dipshit deals."

He sighed. It was one of his better acts. "Ten-thirty," he said.

I walked Anna from Wilma's to her car. Since she'd been in the States, she'd learned to drive and old man Gault had presented her with a new, pale blue BMW.

Her car was parked in a space reserved for the Clerk of Court. A ticket was planted in the windshield wiper on the driver's side.

"When will I see you again, Jim?"

"When a blind hog finds an acorn." A puzzled expression floated across her face. I decided that Poles didn't know how to talk in metaphors.

CHAPTER SEVEN

The spent most of the night sitting at the end of the bar at George's Deli on Highland. When I left the deli, I thought about stopping by Hump's and checking in on him. It was dark on the street. A brisk clammy wind was blowing and I thought it might rain before morning.

I was nearly at my car when I heard car doors open and close and I swung around and faced the street. It was too late. I stared at the two heavies who approached me at a steady pace.

Suckered. I'd been so sure it was over that I'd left my gun in my glove box.

"Mr. Busco wants to see you." The one who spoke was broad across the chest, about two hundred and twenty pounds and he carried about three hundred dollars' worth of suit on his back. His nose had been broken a time or two and nudged toward the left side of his face. His teeth were so good and even I decided they were false. Unless the man who'd broken his nose had been careful to spare his teeth.

The other man was smaller, about my weight. He wore a dark London Fog windbreaker and chinos.

I watched them spread and flank me. "Tell him I regret that I have another appointment. I'm getting my car washed."

The man in the dark windbreaker was so close he didn't have to take a step. He reached me from a flat-footed stance. He hit me a shot in my left kidney and I felt my knees start to buckle under me.

After the smaller man hit me, he stepped forward and caught me and pulled me upright. The big man leaned in and took my other arm. They half-walked, half-dragged me toward a dark Impala parked beside the curb.

The big man blew garlic breath at me. "He said you might try to make excuses. He told us to insist."

I coughed. There was a glob of thick phlegm in the back of my throat. I had to clear that before I could speak. "I've already had the message from his play pretty."

"She is, ain't she?" the big man said.

The little man opened the car door. The big man grabbed me by the back of my coat and rammed me into the far side of the back seat. He pushed in behind me. The little man closed the door. By the time I got myself upright, the little man had started the car engine.

I was worried until I realized we were headed toward Briarcliff. It wasn't going to be a dip in the river after all. At least not right away.

The pain in my left kidney sliced and cut at me. The big man patted me down, neck to ankles. "The nice man doesn't have iron on him," the big man said.

"I like him," the driver said. "In fact, I even liked his friend last night when we met him."

"Lots of quality people in this part of the country," the man beside me said. "Now if a man could find a good onion bagel down here."

Fuck you. Go home, carpetbagger.

That was at the edge of my teeth, about to slip past my mouth. I swallowed it. I decided I might need that kidney when I grew older.

"Meeting quality people is one way of getting an education," the driver said.

The Impala turned onto Briarcliff. The big man said, "I have to admit I like this city of yours."

"I don't own much of it." I said.

"You hear him? You hear the funny man?" The big man laughed. The driver joined in with him. The car slowed and turned in at the driveway of a new condominium. "I like a man who can joke," the big man said. Suddenly, hardly turning in my direction at all, he planted a huge right fist in my left kidney again. I grunted and fell against the far side of the car.

I struggled for breath. "What... what...?"

"That's so you'll remember not to joke with Mr. Busco."

Busco stood at a half circle of a bar on one side of his sunken living room. He was wearing a red jogging outfit with University of Georgia logo on the breast of it and DAWGS in script across the back at the shoulder level. He kept me waiting while he poured Perrier over ice and added a twist of lemon.

I had trouble trying to straighten my back. It wanted to fold forward like a jackknife.

Busco came from behind the bar. He was in socked feet. He carried his Perrier to a chair and sat down and pulled a new pair of Nike jogging shoes toward him. A sip of the Perrier and he slipped his feet into the shoes tied the laces. "You don't look well, Hardman. Perhaps you'd like to jog with me tonight?"

I shook my head. "I'm having trouble with a kidney."

"You got to take care of your body," Busco said. "It's the only one you'll ever have."

"I'm expecting the transplant any day," I said.

The big man on my left turned his head and stared at me. I flinched. Then Busco laughed and the big man relaxed.

"You mind if I sit down?"

"Be comfortable."

"I could use a drink," I said.

Busco nodded at the big man.

"A beer."

When the big man returned from behind the bar, he brought me a San Miguel and a glass. I waved the glass away and gulped it straight from the bottle.

"I'm disappointed, Hardman. I thought I'd sent you a message last night."

"And a message this morning. I got both messages." The San Miguel was strong and hoppy. I felt a big bubble burst in the back of my throat.

"I assumed that two messages would be more than enough."

"I'm out of it," I said.

"But you meddled one last time"

I shook my head. I didn't understand.

"The lawyer. You talked her into seeing Butler this morning."

"I see." I didn't really. "I thought it was better if Mrs. Gault saw Butler and got him off her case. He's a man with a lot of influence."

Busco smiled. It was a smile without humor. "Not anymore. He doesn't have the power anymore."

"There are different kinds of power," I explained. "Muscle, physical clout." I turned my head and looked at the big man. Busco turned his head and followed my direction. "And there is another kind of power. Accumulated political power. A little man like Butler, a man who probably can't lift fifty pounds without getting a hernia. His power comes from knowing where the bodies are buried. Twenty or thirty years of that knowledge." I smiled. "You ever meet him?"

Busco shook his head.

"He's got delicate hands, the hands of a child. But those hands can pull strings from the local level to the state level to the federal level."

"He doesn't scare me." Busco stood and began to do his loosening up exercises.

"I'll tell you what you do." I hooked a thumb toward the big man. "You send him ..."

"Herb," Busco said.

"Send Herb over to hit Frank Butler in the kidney and see what happens."

"An assault charge?"

I shook my head. "Mr. Butler would never admit that he had been assaulted. A week might pass. Perhaps a month. And then the sky would fall on Herb. Something unexpected. He might even find himself charged with something he hadn't done. In no time at all, Herb is doing eight-to-ten. And it will be a full ten. No parole."

Herb didn't like the conversation.

"This talk about kidneys..." Busco tilted his head toward Herb.

"He was cracking wise, Mr. Busco."

"I see."

"I'd just met Herb," I said. "I wanted to see if he had a sense of humor."

"You hold grudges too, Hardman?" Busco did a toe touch, only he placed the palm of his hands on the carpet.

"Not me. If Herb gets the back of his head blown away in the next month or two, you can bet money it'll never be traced to me." I shrugged. "The way I see it, a guy like Herb probably has a lot of people who don't like him."

"You hear that, Herb?"

"Yes, sir."

The pat, pat, pat of Busco's palm on the carpet. Then he straightened his back. He took a swallow of the Perrier. "Anna said you were an odd one."

"That's supposed to be a compliment?"

"I think she meant it that way"

"Enough silly games. What did Anna tell Butler?"

"The truth. That she needed the money above and beyond what was available from the old man."

I'd been sipping at the San Miguel. Another gulp and I emptied the bottle. I took a step toward the bar. The big man, Herb, blocked my wav. I handed him the beer bottle. "If I know Butler the next question is..."

"Anna told him she needed the money to help her relatives in Poland."

"Is that true?"

"It's as true as anything else," Busco said. "There are a lot of wells a woman can throw twenty-five big ones down. Poland is as good a well as any."

"What are some of the other wells?"

"Too many to list." He shook his head.

"Is Anna in trouble?"

"There are a number of kinds of trouble."

"I think we've had this conversation." I tried to turn too abruptly. The left kidney clawed at me. I hit on my bottom lip until the pain eased.

"When you're ready, Paul will drive you home." Busco nodded at the smaller man.

"I'm almost ready." I took a deep breath. "I'm puzzled. All this trouble and I still don't know why I'm here."

"I wanted to meet you. Say I was curious."

The driver, Paul, led me toward the door. In the doorway, with Paul behind me in the hall, I turned back to Busco. "You'd tell me if Anna was in any trouble?"

"It wouldn't be any of your business."

I backed through the doorway. Paul stepped past me and closed the apartment door.

"Try the cops." I got to my feet slowly. I put most of my weight on the kitchen table. I rubbed my left kidney.

"I smell a lie." Frank Butler sat across from me at my kitchen table. It was a mark of how important this was that he'd come to my house when I said I was under the weather a bit and couldn't go to his office. "I know a lie when I smell one."

"Call the police. Call the F.B.I."

"You're no help, Jim."

"You'll have to forgive me," I said. "I could have used help getting out of bed this morning. And *that* was just so Busco could meet me."

Butler closed his eyes and rubbed his perfectly shaved chin. "Tell me which bad boy hurt your kidney."

"Not this time. I will if he does it again."

"Scruples, Jim?"

"I don't want this to become an open war."

He sighed. It was deep, full of disappointment. "You think Anna might talk to you?"

"Maybe. She has so far."

"Dammit, Jim, I can't fight shadows. I've got to know what's going on with her. I don't see Harrison Gault living much longer. When he dies, the boy inherits it all. Well, most of it. It will be years before the boy is old enough to manage the estate himself. That leaves it to Anna and to me. I've got to know if I've got to worry about Anna."

"It could be fucking," I said. "Maybe Anna can't tell the difference between fucking a hood from New Jersey and a graduate of Princeton."

"The money," Butler said impatiently, "the money."

"I'll talk to her."

"I'll arrange it."

"I don't need..."

"Gault's been asking about you. There's a dinner at Gault Farm Saturday night. You're invited and you're to stay the night."

"Me at Gault Farm?"

He nodded and handed me an engraved invitation, the date and the times written in with a thick, sure hand. Cocktails at seven, Dinner at eight. The Gault Farm, Gaultsville, Georgia.

"Anna will be there playing hostess for him."

"Is Busco invited?"

"Don't be silly, Jim."

❖   ❖   ❖

The Gault Farm was famous in Georgia. It had been a small home-stead, forty acres and two mules from Revolutionary days until about the turn of the century. Around 1900, Harrison Gault's father, Amos, went into the meat business. Gault Farm hams and sausage and bacon. The salt-cured hams that were dark as dried blood, link sausage and bulk, and bacon sliced an eighth-of-an-inch thick. There were no shortcuts. All the products were prepared the way they'd been done for hundreds of years. Real smoke, not liquid smoke. The hams packed in salt rather than injected with a saline solution.

When the Depression came, Amos had ready money. Almost none of his neighbors did. By the time Harrison Gault, the son, moved into the Governor's mansion, Amos had bought most of the good farm land around his original forty acres. He stopped at six hundred acres, give or take a half acre or so.

Amos died. World War Two began. Harrison took over the Farm. He seemed to know how to make money breed more money. Harrison speculated in land, he owned a construction company and his meat products company thrived.

The war ended. Gault Farm had changed with the times. The Farm didn't raise their own hogs anymore. They bought at the hog markets. The bacon, the sausage and most of the hams were prepared and cured at a bright modern plant in Gaultsville. Perhaps for the memory, to keep the tradition alive, a thousand hams were salt-cured a year on the Farm in the old way, packed in salt and slowly air dried in the smokehouse from the winter until the end of the following summer. These were the "One of a Thousand" hams. Across the state, across the southeast, these hams were tracked down and bought and treasured. From the first slice until the bone simmered in a huge pot of pinto beans.

The packaging for Gault Farm meats hadn't changed in eighty years. White wrapping paper was used, a reminder of butcher paper, and the logo was a faded old photo of a stern-looking Amos staring out at the buyer. Under that the simple slogan, *Country Good.*

I figured it for a three-hour drive. A loop down to the southeast that carried me through beautiful countryside. The leaves were changing, fingerprints of gold and red, and the land was chilling now for the winter that would come.

When I reached Gaultsville, I saw it for what it was. A company town. Not like in the old days, in the really bad sense. It was, however, a one industry town. You lived there, you either worked for the packing company or you furnished some essential service for the people who worked there.

It was a small town, hardly a bump on the edge of my eyes as I passed through and headed for the Farm. I knew I was almost there when I saw the freshly painted white board fence and a pasture beyond where a couple of mares and their colts trotted and frisked about. The board fence seemed to run around half-a-mile before I reached the gate. When I stopped at the gate, I checked my watch. It was five after seven. The cocktail hour, as promised on the invitation, was underway.

A private security guard stood on the highway side of the gate. I hadn't known whether I was expected to bring my invitation with me. I reached for the glove box before I saw the guard carried a clipboard with him. I dropped my hand and relaxed.

"Your name, sir?"

I told him. He checked it against the list on the clipboard. He nodded and opened the gate for me. I drove past a jeep with GAULT FARMS on the side of it, a rack with an M-16 lodged in it behind the seatback and an antenna whip tied in place over the left rear wheel.

The manor house was straight ahead. The same kind of white board fence bordered each side of the driveway. One of the colts stuck his head between the boards and watched me go by. The house was large and white, with black trim, with porch columns so big a man couldn't reach around them and a high, rounded arch above the entranceway. The wide steps to the front porch were of old brick, slave-made brick I read in an article somewhere, and gleaming polished rocking chairs were motionless on the porch.

I made my turn and started to drive past the front of the house. I was looking for parking. A young black man in a red cutaway jacket, dark trousers and polished black shoes came around the side of the house and waved an arm. at me. I stopped. As he walked toward me, he brought a folded sheet of paper from his hip pocket. "I'll park it for you, sir."

I slid from the seat, leaving the keys in the ignition.

"What is your name, sir?"

I told him.

"Your bag?"

"On the back seat," I said.

"I'll see it gets to your room."

As he passed me, about to enter my car, I reached into my pocket and brought out a couple of ones. He almost jumped a foot in the air. "Oh, no, sir. It ain't necessary, sir." As he spoke, he looked toward the house, as if frightened.

I thanked him instead.

He relaxed and grinned at me.

A black butler, gray-haired and sprightly, as if he'd come from some movie casting company, opened the door for me even before I touched the doorbell. "The other guests are through there, sir," he said.

I adjusted my tie and walked down the hall. The floor had a shine like glass and it felt as slick as glass. Past the hall, there was a wide, high-ceilinged anteroom. To the right, was a curving staircase that led to the second floor. I followed the sound of voices to my left and found myself in a living room or a library or a combination of both. Roughly a dozen people were in a room large enough to handle four times that many without crowding.

Heads turned toward me when I stopped in the entranceway. There had been a silence, a break, and now a recording of
a string quartet started up from a hidden sound system. I heard
just enough of it to guess that it was Bartók. Voices mixed in with
the instruments and spoiled it. At first glance around the room,
I saw two people I knew. I moved toward Frank Butler. Beyond
him. I saw Anna.

Butler met me, his hand extended. "Glad you could
come, Jim."

He guided me toward the bar. Another young black man, also
in a red cutaway jacket, mixed me a scotch over ice. I had a sip. A
single malt. One I didn't recognize by the flavor. Frank allowed
another swallow and then he escorted me on a slow circuit of
the room. The Lieutenant Governor was there, a porky man with
flabby jowls and a new hair transplant that he'd insisted on after
he read somewhere that bald politicians didn't stand a chance at
the polls anymore. His wife was blonde and had hair that looked
plastic. She looked about fifteen years younger than he did. She
was restless and uneasy. This one, I told myself as I shook her
perfumed hand, needs careful watching. A man didn't want to
meet her in a dark hall unless he wanted to grope and be groped.

Other names, other faces. I met a writer who lived on
St. Simon. His last book had been a Korean war novel. He was
the sort of person Marcy would be impressed to see me talking to. But I hadn't read his book so he wasn't interested in me.
A very young girl, his secretary he said, held his elbow like she
thought he might fall through the floor. I didn't know writers
had secretaries.

Small talk, useless talk. I took a deep breath after I cleared
the mob and reached the far corner where Anna stood. She put
her arms around me and hugged me. A kiss at the corner of my
mouth tasted of vodka. "You see? I said I would arrange for you
to come and visit me."

I said she was exactly one hundred percent right.

"You will have to meet little Harry later. He is in bed now. Perhaps it would be better in the morning."

"I'll look forward to it," I said.

She smiled. "You don't know how happy I am to see you again, Miami."

"It's only been a few days."

"That was not social." She lifted her hand and I saw that she was directing my attention. The emerald and diamond choker was at her throat. "Thank you."

"For what?"

She moved her head from side-to-side, rapidly. "Oh, you."

"I don't accept misdirected thanks."

"Then I thank you for not bringing a woman with you. I have arranged that you are my escort tonight."

"I couldn't do better." She did look good. I was getting used to the tan. The dark gray evening dress was form-fitting and the skirt was slit up the front, almost to the crotch.

Frank Butler touched my arm. "Let me have him for a few minutes, Anna."

"I lend him to you," Anna said. She laughed and moved away.

"Harrison wants to meet you."

I looked around the huge room. He wasn't here unless he'd just entered. "I don't see …"

"He's in his office."

On the way through the room we stopped at the bar. Butler left his glass there. I waited long enough for the bartender to pour me another single malt scotch over ice.

The office was dimly lit. A single lamp in a far corner furnished most of the lighting. The drapes were open, revealing a large picture window that covered most of one wall. But it was almost dark outside. From that window, the room looked out on a fenced-in area, a corral. A large stud Morgan was alone in the corral. It moved, it was restless, as if it knew he was being watched.

"Harrison, this is Jim Hardman."

He sat in a wheelchair. His head was massive, topped by a wild stand of gray hair. What had been a strong body was wasted now, only what remained of the bones and the skin that held those bones together.

His handshake was cool and weak. I touched his hand, held it a bit longer than I wanted to, and stepped away. His voice was stronger and deeper than I expected it to be. "I have heard many things about you, Jim."

"Good or bad?"

"Both." He smiled. "I'm too old to have to lie to people anymore."

"I envy you. I have to lie all the time."

"As long as it's for business, young man, and not for pleasure."

"Mostly business," I said.

Harrison Gault peered into my glass. "Is that what I think it is?" He extended a hand and I passed the glass to him. He held the glass to the light and then he sniffed the drink. "I can't drink anymore. There are so many things I can't do I'm beginning to wonder if this isn't some kind of preparation for dying." He returned my glass to me. "The single malt?"

I nodded. "An excellent one."

"It was my drink when I could still drink."

I took a sip and let it settle on my tongue before I swallowed. "I don't recognize it."

"I'd he more surprised if you did. It's Clynelesh, from Brora, Scotland. A hotel there in town gets a few barrels from the distillery. What they don't sell in the public house at the Royal Mariner is bottled and selected friends are notified. I was once one of those selected friends. An English lawyer handled it for me. Twelve bottles a year."

"It's an odd choice for a bar whiskey for a cocktail party."

"Oh, it's not." Gault lifted his head slowly and laughed. "If any of those rednecks are drinking my Clynelesh, I'll fire the bartender."

"A treat for me?"

"I knew it wouldn't be wasted on you," he said. "If there's a spare bottle in the cellar, I'll present you with it to take back to Atlanta."

"I won't waste it." With all the talk I realized that there had been nothing from Frank Butler. I turned and looked behind me. He'd disappeared without a word and closed the door behind him. "I didn't know Frank could do a magic vanishing act."

"He waited until he was sure we weren't going to throw fists at each other."

"I don't have any reason to throw anything at you."

"A figure of speech." He indicated a straight-backed chair near the door. "Bring that closer."

I placed the chair directly in front of him, about four feet away. In the corral, the Morgan pawed the earth with a right, front hoof, as if to show he could count to a hundred.

"I respect Frank's judgment. He trusts you."

I sipped the Clynelesh.

"You handled a difficult job in London. Another man might have dropped it and returned and said that Harry had disappeared and that was all there was to it."

"It only called for a certain amount of lower grade lying."

He laughed, this time under control. Laughing seemed to tire him more than talking. "It was a painful business for me. I can't tell you how painful. But I am happy with little Harry. He's his daddy all over again."

I was listening. I was accustomed to the dim light now.

My eyes roved over the room. I recognized a big tintype on the wall behind a desk. It was the picture of old Amos Gault that was used on all the Gault Farm meat packages.

"I asked you here to talk about Anna."

"That's a hard one," I said.

"Frank doesn't lie to me. I hope you won't either."

"I don't know what Frank has told you." Far under my breath I cursed Butler. The least he could have done was brief me on how much he'd told the old man. Without that, I didn't know how much he knew about the emerald and diamond choker.

"I know she has involved herself with a man who has an unsavory reputation. Hell, let's call it what it is. The man's no more than a gangster."

"He's all of that."

"You've met him?"

"Once," I said, "and that was one time too many."

"Yes?"

"He plays rough."

"Why would she become involved with a man like him?"

"It's a new world for her. Maybe she doesn't know any better."

"She respects you, Jim."

I laughed. "What do you know about me?"

"How you left the police force under a cloud and how you make your living now."

"She likes me. She's involved with a hood. Maybe she's got a taste for the wrong kind of man."

"You're hard on yourself," he said.

I shrugged. It was how Marcy thought of me. It was how Art and his wife looked at me. The only one who didn't share that sentiment was Hump. I didn't want to argue the point. It wasn't my business to prove to him how tainted I was.

"Anna's been a comfort to me. The boy too. But I'll be damned before I let all that my daddy worked for, and all I worked for, for fall into the hands of some scum from the north."

"There are ways Frank can protect the estate."

"He's explained the options to me."

I could guess some of them. Trust funds. A set income for the mother so that she would not want for anything. Most of the estate protected from any pillaging by the boy's mother or by any husband she might take.

"What I really want," Gault said, "is Busco, out of her life."

"Frank's your man for that, too."

"I need an opinion from you. I don't know Busco, and Frank doesn't know him, either. I guess what I'm asking is whether Busco is a man I ought to worry about."

"I'd worry about him if I were you."

"Enough to find some way of clearing him out of the state of Georgia?"

"I thought I could get away with it, I would put a .357 round up his nose."

"Thank you, Jim. I've been called a ruthless man, but I've always wanted to be certain I had about forty percent of the right on my side before I acted."

I stood. I moved the chair back beside the door. Harrison Gault wheeled his chair past me and sat there, with his nose almost pressed against the glass of the picture window. The Morgan stud sensed he was there and turned and trotted to the corral fence near the window. The horse stood there, shaking the muscles of his shoulders and looking at Gault.

"I'll see you at dinner," Gault said.

I returned to the cocktail party. It was almost over. I had time for one more Clynelesh before dinner was served.

CHAPTER EIGHT

After dinner, there was coffee and a choice of brandies and Cuban cigars in the library. The women, except for Anna, had been escorted into a small sitting room off the anteroom. Anna remained with the men and served the coffee and poured the brandy. She'd even lit a Cuban cigar for Harrison Gault and allowed him three or four puffs before she took it from him and took a playful drag on it herself.

"All for you," she told Gault.

Gault protested but it was more in fun than anything else. Anna placed the cigar in an ashtray and brought a decanter across the room to me. "I remembered that you like calvados."

Gault watched us from a distance. "I wondered who drank that vile stuff."

I lowered an eye toward him. "In that case, make it a double."

Anna let me finish my brandy. She waited until my coffee cup was empty. All around us the talk was of taxes and interest, of factoring, of stocks that split, of mergers. I felt out of place and restless.

Anna took my elbow and moved me across the library until we stood in front of old Gault. "I am taking Jim to the nursery to introduce him to Harry," Anna said.

"Do that," Gault said. "A few more minutes of this business and I wouldn't be surprised if we drove Mr. Hardman back to Atlanta tonight."

We climbed the curving staircase. There was a hallway at the top of the stairs. We followed that and worked our way into a wing at the left rear of the house. As soon as we were close to it, I could smell the nursery. It had a scent of talcum and baby oils and lotions and disinfectant sprays.

Anna opened the door. A grandmotherly black woman with gray hair sat beside the crib. She wore a dark blue uniform dress. Her head was down, over an open Bible. She heard us and got to her feet quickly.

"Bea, this is Mr. Hardman."

"Yes ma'am."

I caught a glimpse of her eyes. They seemed red and tired.

"How is Harry?"

"Sleeping like a cat," Bea said. She turned and moved toward a door to the side of the nursery, "You call me when you want me, Miss Gault." She entered a room that connected to the baby's room and closed the door behind her.

Anna pulled me toward the crib. I remembered the picture of Harry Gault that I had taken to London with me. It was the same face, the exact bone structure. The hair was different. The baby had Anna's crow-wing colored hair.

"Is he not beautiful, Miami?"

"Beautiful," I said.

"Oh, you." Anna pouted. "You always make fun of me."

"Your hair and Harry's face," I said. "It could have been the other way around."

She wasn't listening. I hadn't realized how close we were to each other. The air seemed electric around us. When she turned to me, I put up my arms, my hands on her shoulders, to hold her away. When she moved forward, there didn't seem to be much strength in my arms. She saw me for what I was and it didn't repulse her. She didn't care if I had a good job or not. That made her a bad judge of character.

"Watch it," I whispered. "Harry is going to know more than he ought to at his age."

"Yes," The pout faded from her mouth. Her mouth when I kissed her, was sweet with brandy and I could feel the heat that ran the length of her. Her right hand moved down my side. Before I knew what was happening, her hand stroked the front of my fly. I felt myself hardening. "I think you like me also, Miami, but you pretend that you do not."

"That's true."

"Why do you pretend ...?"

I backed away "Let's go downstairs. I need a drink."

"Now you have made me truly angry." Anna whirled away from me. She tapped lightly on the door connected to the nursery, "Bea?"

The door opened almost immediately. The little black woman entered, still carrying her Bible. When she passed me her eyes brushed against me. Tired yes. I wondered when she'd last slept for six or seven hours.

"I'll look in later," Anna said.

"Yes ma'am."

I stopped in the hallway. Anna closed the door after us. "Do you think you could find the nursery later tonight?"

I said I thought I could.

Anna pointed toward a closed door down the hall from the nursery on the left. "My suite of rooms is there."

I wondered if I'd make the trip to those doors. We returned to the library to join the other guests.

"Come in, Jim."

Anna was in a sheer white robe, seated on the side of the bed, turned slightly away from me when I entered two hours later in a bathrobe, pajamas and bedroom slippers. She hunched over something on the top of the table beside her bed. I walked around the bed and stood behind her.

I recognized the package first. The white package with the blue seal on it and the plastic outer bag with the lumps of desiccant in the bottom of it.

There was a square of paper on the table, a piece about the size for a hamburger patty. While I watched, she cut the lumps with a single-edged razor, the kind that is used mainly now to scraps paint from glass.

I leaned forward and lifted the package. A gram, two grams, worth a hundred dollars or better a gram, according to the purity.

"Peruvian cocaine," Anna said. "Some of the best there is. Do you like it?"

"I don't think I've had Peruvian," I said. I dropped the package on the table top. In fact, I'd had little cocaine at all. Once at a party. What was it the French writer had said? *Once a scientist. Twice a pervert.* But he was talking about Arab boys another writer had furnished him. I'd thought of that quote the one time I'd done cocaine. That and what a friend who'd spent twenty-five thousand on it over a year and a half had said. "The nose is the human body's largest opening. You can suck a house, a car, a wife and a bank account up it without noticing the least discomfort."

Chop, chop, chop. Anna broke the cocaine lumps. When there were no more lumps, she used the edge of the blade to divide the cocaine into thin strings of powder. "I will go first," she said. She took what looked to be a small cocktail straw from the back of the table and placed it at the bottom end of the first of the four strings of powder. She leaned forward and snorted that cocaine row into her right nostril. She turned and offered the straw to me.

"Not just yet," I said. "It might dim my performance."

"We wouldn't want that, Miami." She smiled and placed the tip Of the Straw on the bottom of the second string and walked the straw up the row until it disappeared into her left nostril "Now," she said, "now." She dropped the straw and stood. Her robe fell and she was naked under it. She grabbed my robe and helped me remove it. Even before she tugged my pajama bottoms to my ankles she was on her knees on the rug, grabbing at me with both hands.

There was a low wattage light in a lamp across the bedroom. I stretched out on the bed beside Anna, hands behind my head. There was a light, feathery snore from Anna. A faucet dripped in the bathroom.

The cocaine. That was the well. Not that any one person could use that much on herself. Usually there was company, others who snorted a ten dollar bill up each nostril and hardly had the breath or the mind left to say thanks. No, one person couldn't pour twenty-five thousand down the well in such a short time. Not in the short time since she'd had Harry and was out and about in Atlanta.

There were lots of wells, Carl Busco had said. One well is just like another one. I had the feeling that Busco knew all the wells by name and serial number. His wells, the wells he'd helped dig. And he'd probably put his bucket in the bottom of the wells so he caught a part of what fell in. Or was tossed in.

I turned on my hip and looked at Anna. The sex was okay. I was a spy who'd found out what I wanted to know, that cocaine was part of the well. I'd done my multiplication tables backwards in my mind until I knew that I wouldn't lose it early and then, when I knew that she was happy, I'd said fuck it and let the math go.

Still a spy. A spy in the bedroom.

I eased my weight from the bed. I dressed and found one-bedroom slipper under the bed. I belted my robe. By my watch, it was after four a.m. I started for the door. As an afterthought, I returned and took the sheet of paper from the bedside table. I folded it so that I wouldn't spill the cocaine that remained on it, the final two strings. I put the paper carefully into my robe pocket and left Anna's bedroom.

I was level with the nursery when I heard the low sound. It wasn't like anything human. It was a whine and a chant and part of a smothered scream. I moved to the door and put an ear against the wood. I could hear the same sound, magnified now, and I grabbed the door knob and tried it. It turned. I eased the door open and stepped into the nursery.

What I saw stunned me. The old black woman, Bea, now dressed in a full-length flannel nightgown, hovered over the baby's crib. The chanting and the almost animal sounds came from somewhere deep inside her. Her right arm was high and I saw the gleam before I realized that she held a large knife in that hand.

"The devil's ... his spawn ... seven times seven times seven ..."

My bedroom slippers were quiet on the wooden floor. I took two steps. Stopped. Then another step. The fourth step and a board squeaked under my weight. Her head lifted, alert and aware.

"Bea, give me that."

"I can't. He's got the devil's foot."

I managed another step while I shook my head. Disagreeing with her seemed to still her for that moment.

"I swear it. See here. You see." Her left hand jerked at the thin blanket that covered Harry.

"I don't see anything." I took another step.

"The Lord done told me to do it," Bea said. "He come to me in a dream."

"Show me what you're talking about." I'd reached the end of the crib. I was within an arm's distance of Bea. Now I'd have to wait for my chance. If I couldn't talk her into giving me the knife.

The baby, Harry, awoke. His first bellow startled me. Bea's head jerked away from me. She stared down at the baby with a mixture of horror and fascination. Her right hand, which had relaxed the more I talked to her, now moved, high above her shoulder. "He knows," she hissed. "The devil knows."

I didn't have time to talk anymore. I lunged around the end of the crib. I barged against her and my right hand reached for the arm that held the knife. I got my first surprise then. For her size, for her age, she was amazingly strong. Perhaps it was a strength that came from her madness, her insanity. The knife hand swung downward. All I could do was deflect it so that the blade slashed into the left side of the crib mattress.

I slid my hand down Bea's arm and made a grab for her wrist. Somehow the wrist eluded me and I felt my hand slide along the blade edge of the knife. It cut deep, a burn at first, and I finally decided to hell with this. I rammed a shoulder into the little woman and pushed her against the wall. I shook the crib doing it and Harry screamed louder and louder. Bea crumpled against the wall and slumped to a sitting position. Her head fell into her hands and she sobbed.

I lifted the hem of my bathrobe and wrapped the cloth around my cut hand. I heard running footsteps approaching the nursery. Frank Butler, out of breath, exploded through the doorway. His eyes from me to the old woman and then to the crib. "What the hell?"

I reached into the crib and withdrew the knife from the place where it was lodged in the mattress. "Bea wanted to kill little Harry."

"Why?"

I looked down at the crying baby Harry's feet were uncovered now. The right foot was webbed between the middle toe and the ones on both side of it. "She said something about him having the devil's foot."

"That?" Frank stared at the little woman in disbelief. "She knows the foot's going to be operated on in the next month."

I passed the knife to Frank. "Take care of this." I used my good hand to cover the baby. Anna ran screaming into the room. I stepped aside to let her reach down into the crib and scoop the baby into her arms. "Take the baby to your room, please," I said to her. "Go ahead." I gave her shoulder a gentle push. "I'll stop in and talk to you later."

"You promise?"

I promised.

"Hush, baby Harry." Anna soothed him as she walked down the hallway to her room. I heard the crying until the door slammed closed to her bedroom,

Bea lifted her face from her hands. "Kill me, mister."

"No," I said. "It's not your fault."

"I beg you to."

I shook my head. "We'll get you some help," I said.

There was a phone in Bea's room. Frank used it to call the security booth near the front gate. The guard arrived a couple of minutes later while Butler was placing a call to Dr. Ethan Bates. I heard only the loud part of the conversation with Dr. Bates. Frank said, "I don't care what time it is. You get your fat ass over here right now."

Frank brought a terrycloth robe from the bedroom. He helped Bea to her feet and he and the guard adjusted the robe on her and belted it. "Dr. Bates is on his way. You stay with Bea until he arrives."

The guard put an arm around Bea and led her away.

"Let me show you something, Jim."

I followed him into the small neat room. The bed hadn't been slept in. The Bible was open on one of the pillows. "These," Butler said. He reached into the trashcan and brought out two medicine bottles. I read the labels. Paregoric. The cure-all mothers used to give their babies for croup and teething pain and anything else that bothered them. Tincture of opium. The paregoric was, according to the labels, prescribed by Dr. Ethan Bates. I unscrewed one of the caps and sniffed it. It brought back a memory. Some childhood illness that I'd forgotten.

I dropped the bottles into the trashcan. Hell, I thought, the whole damned house is on dope.

For the first time Frank seemed to notice that I had part of the robe wrapped around my right hand. "What's that?"

"A cut."

"Let me see." He unwrapped the robe. One whole section of the cloth was soaked in my blood, I'd made a fist with the hand. It clenched that way. It took both of his hands to open the balled-up hand. He stared at it and whistled under his breath. "A cut? It looks like the Suez Canal."

He led me down the hall to his room. He looked in the medicine cabinet in the bathroom and found nothing he could use. He found a clean pillowcase in one of the closets and tore it into strips and wrapped my hand.

"You didn't mention exactly how you happened to be in that wing of the house."

"No, I didn't."

I had trouble reaching across my body. I jerked the robe around until I could get my left hand into the right-hand pocket. I pulled out the folded packet and handed it to Butler. "Don't spill it."

He opened the folds carefully. "What is it?"

"Coke."

"Where'd you get it?"

"One guess."

"Anna?"

"That's where part of the money went. It's an expensive hobby."

"Busco?"

"Very likely," I said.

I stood in the doorway of Anna's room. She sat on the edge of her rumpled bed. The sheets twisted at the foot of the bed. Harry was sleeping again, braced against her hip.

Her face was slack, drained. "Why did Bea try to do this, Jim?"

"Warped religion," I said. "She kept saying he had the devil's foot."

"She loved Harry."

"The dope too."

"What?"

"Paregoric. Usually you'd expect paregoric to make a person sleepy, drowsy. Lord knows what happens when you mix it with insanity and lack of sleep and bad dreams."

"I got the paregoric for her. She said she needed it to help her sleep."

"Through Dr. Bates?"

"Yes. I told him I needed it for Harry."

"A bad business." I was tired, my mind felt numb, and the hand throbbed.

"Poor, poor Bea."

I shook my head slowly from side-to-side. It was getting harder and harder to understand Anna. I said I'd see her later.

It turned out I didn't. Not that night. Dr. Bates, when he arrived, took one look at the deep cut in the palm of my hand. He rushed into the other room to call a surgeon he knew in Atlanta. He arranged an operation at Georgia Baptist for later that morning. I dressed while Frank Butler packed for me.

Charles, the young black man who'd parked my car for me before the dinner party, drove me to Atlanta in my car. I huddled on the passenger side of the front seat, the hurt hand cradled against my chest and my shoulder braced against the locked door. I wasn't feeling any pain now. Dr. Bates had given me some kind of painkiller and told me to take one. I'd taken two and now I drifted in and out of the fog. Part of the time, I knew where I was and part of the time I was lost. I must have been doing some talking. I remember Charles turning to me several times and saying, "Sir? Sir?"

We arrived at Georgia Baptist before the surgeon did. I found a pay phone and called Hump and got him out of bed. He showed up a quarter of an hour later at the emergency room. I made my arrangements with Hump before a nurse wheeled me away to the operating room. He'd lead Charles to my house and see that my car was parked. Then he'd take Charles to the bus station downtown. From there, Charles would take a bus back to Gaultsville. I pressed two twenties on Charles. He still didn't want to take money from me. I insisted. "It's between us. There's no law says you can't have a good breakfast before you take the bus."

I convinced him or he allowed me to.

The nurse wheeled me down the corridors of the hospital. My head was full of weird dreams, dreams I knew I dreamed but could not remember when I opened my eyes.

I was in the operating room for almost two hours.

CHAPTER NINE

Frank Butler arrived the day after the operation. "I dropped a bottle off at your house this morning. Left it on your back step."

"Bottle?"

"The Clynelesh you liked so much. Harrison insisted I deliver a bottle to you from him."

"Thank him for me."

"He said I was to thank you."

"It's a thank-you standoff then."

Butler carried a briefcase with him. I remember thinking that was odd of him. He could have left his business papers locked in his car in the lot. After some general talk he was ready to leave. The room was empty. The nurse had passed through and closed the door behind her. Butler snapped the catches on his briefcase and took out a glass flask with a silver top. It was filled to the cap with a brown liquid. "The best I could find on short notice." he explained. "Glenlivet."

I thanked him for being thoughtful and placed the glass flask under the covers, next to my left hip.

Hump came by at five and dropped a Blue Streak edition of *The Atlanta Journal* on my chest.

"Interesting reading on the front page," he said. I shared my flask with him and he took a pull while I read.

The main headline, the banner, announced a big drug bust in the city. In the story under that, it was revealed that the federal branch, the D.E.A., and the Georgia S.B.I., working together, had closed down a drug network that channeled a variety of illegal drugs across the southeast. There had been a number of arrests, other arrests were expected, and a sizable amount of drugs and cash had been confiscated.

"Check the names," Hump said.

I did. I skipped a paragraph. I found the one that interested me. Carl Busco. He was rumored to be the kingpin of the drug ring.

"Gets you right there, doesn't it?" Hump tapped his heart.

I said it did.

Early the next morning, before I checked out of the hospital, a nice potted plant arrived, sent by the Gault family. I carried it home with me and put it in a window where it would receive enough light. I watered it. I even tried talking to it. Within the week, it withered and died.

Carl Busco appeared in court and posted two hundred thousand dollars bail in cash, and was released pending his trial. Within an hour, Busco jumped bail and dropped out of sight. According to Hump, who'd heard it from The Man, the rumors on the street were that Carl Busco had left the state and was hiding in New Jersey.

Three slow weeks passed, and I hardly thought about Anna or the Gaults at all. I thought about Marcy, though. I wondered if she was happy. When I found myself on the edge of calling her, Claudia, the madam I knew, got a call from me instead. She'd send a girl over. It only made me feel worse.

It was fall. The weathergirl on TV said it was going to be one of the better weekends to visit the mountains and see all the trees in their fall splendor. It was tempting. I almost weakened until I thought of all the other idiots in the area who'd heard the same weathergirl. I decided to stay in the city. The mountains, this weekend, were going to be as crowded as one of those northern turnpikes during Labor Day.

I tinkered around the house all morning. Sooner or later I'd have to install the storm windows. The eyesore lawn waited for me to decide whether I was going to rake it or cover it with green concrete.

The phone rang around noon. I was in the kitchen sipping a cup of tomato soup. The voice was that of a black man. "Mr. Hardman? Is that you?"

"Yeah."

"This is me. Charles. I drove you back from Gaultsville the night you were cut."

"Sure, I remember you."

"Well, Mr. Hardman, I got this problem and I don't know what to do about it."

"Where are you now, Charles?"

"At a phone booth on Highland. I didn't want to come by without you expecting me."

"You remember which house is mine?"

"I think so."

I counted the houses from the corner for him and told him to come on over. I finished the soup and rinsed the cup before he arrived. I heard a car pull to the curb outside. I went to the window. It was a new blue BMW and I guessed that it was the one that belonged to Anna.

I met him at the door and waved him inside.

"I'm sorry to bother you…"

I stopped him. "Too early for a beer? I'm having one."

"Then I'll have one with you," he said.

He followed me into the kitchen. I got two throwaway Buds from the refrigerator and twisted the caps. I handed one to him and stood back and took a long look at him. It was, in some ways, my first real look at him. The moment in front of the Gault house, when he'd parked my car, had been a brief one. The other time, the drive back to Atlanta, I'd been so doped up I didn't remember much of it.

I put his age at about twenty-five. He was neatly barbered, hair cut short and shaved skin tight around the edges. His trousers and his shirt were J.C. Penney work clothing but neat and pressed. He smelled of some dime store shaving lotion like Aqua Velva.

"What's the problem?"

"It's Miss Anna."

I thought about going down the back steps and putting myself in a garbage can and pulling the lid over me. There had to be a limit somewhere. Every time I got the scent of her washed off me, somebody opened my door and dragged her across my rug. I wanted to say something like that, I wanted to show Charles where the door was. But I couldn't. He was so damned concerned. Seeing how he was, I almost forgot about how much the kidney had hurt and how my right hand didn't have all the strength back yet.

"What about her?"

"I can't find her, Hr. Hardman."

I motioned him to a chair at the kitchen table. He told me about it in spurts and gasps. About a week ago, the Gaults decided to go ahead with the operation on little Harry's foot. Charles was assigned to drive Anna and the baby to Atlanta. They arrived early on Sunday morning. She checked in at the Peachtree Plaza and he helped her take her things to her room. Then he'd driven them to Grady Hospital. His instructions, as they had been the time he'd driven me to the city, were that he was to take the bus back to Gaultsville. At the last minute, because she was going to spend so much time at the hospital, Ann decided that she really didn't need her car. She told him to drive it home and come back for her on Saturday. That was today.

"When was the operation?"

"Monday."

It seemed a short time for a recovery. I said so.

"Miss Anna said it wasn't any hard operation." The doctor had said that she could take the baby hone where he'd be under the care of Dr. Bates. A week later, Anna was to bring Harry back to Grady for a follow-up to the operation.

So far, it was a straightforward tale. I had trouble, jumping ahead of Charles, figuring out what the problem was.

"Only..."

"Yeah?"

"Miss Anna ain't been at the hotel for two nights and the nurses at the hospital say she ain't been there to see the baby since Thursday. In the morning, one of them said."

"You call Mr. Butler?"

"I wasn't told to."

"You call Mr. Gault?"

He shook his head. "I didn't know if I ought to."

I realized what I was up against then. It was some odd kind of loyalty to Anna. Charles thought if he called Butler or Mr. Gault, he'd be getting Anna into trouble. He was probably right about that. Since he didn't think he could call them with his problem, that left me. "Why'd you come to me, Charles?"

"I know she likes you. She told me."

"You could get yourself in trouble, trying to protect her."

"I can't help that, Mr. Hardman. She's been good to me and she's been good to my grandmama."

"Your grandmama?"

"Miss Bea."

I blinked when he looked down at my right hand.

"Miss Bea's the one you kept from hurting the baby."

Jesus Christ. "How is your grandmama?"

"She's at the hospital at Milledgeville. Miss Anna went with me to see her and she took grandmama some bedclothes she needed."

There was no reason for me to be surprised. Whole families worked for companies and farms. Two and three generations. It wasn't slavery the way it was two hundred years ago. This was economic slavery. Charles parked cars and did other work around the Gault Farm and his mother probably cooked or cleaned and his grandmother did the odd jobs as they came up, like taking care of the new baby in the house.

"You have a place to stay in town?"

He shook his head.

"I don't know how long this'll take. My couch is yours. Help yourself to anything you want in the refrigerator. Take a nap or watch TV." I switched on the television set and found the pre-game show before the Game of the Week.

I left him seated in front of the TV. I unplugged the phone and carried it into the bedroom. I inserted the jack and dialed the unlisted number Frank Butler had given me the time I was in London.

"Anna's missing," I said.

There was a long silence at the other end of the line.

"That Goddamn woman," Butler said finally.

The security man at the Peachtree Plaza led Frank Butler and me to Anna's room on the eleventh floor. I could only imagine the clout Butler had to get the security man to do this.

Down the hallway, a black girl pushed a cart piled high with fresh linen and folded towels. The security man left us and talked with the girl for a short time. When he finished with her, he gestured toward Butler and led us to the door to room 1111.

He opened the door with a master key. "The maid says she's cleaned this room all week. The bed hasn't been slept in since Wednesday night. And nothing's been used since she cleaned the room Thursday noon."

I checked the closet first. There were two suitcases and an overnight bag on the floor of the closet. The hangers held dresses, skirts and designer jeans. On the way past the dresser I took a quick look. Underwear, stockings and blouses, plenty of them.

I followed Butler and the security man into the bathroom. The towels were neat, folded and untouched. The washcloths as well. The soap was still wrapped on the wash basin. I leaned around the security man and noted the deodorant, the perfumes, the woman's razor, and the assortment of creams and lotions in the medicine cabinet.

"You going to call the police?" The security man asked his question of me. I avoided it by nodding toward Butler.

"Not yet," Butler said. "We don't want to embarrass the Gault family if we can help it."

The security man counted it off on his fingers. "Thursday, Friday and part of today. I was a cop for eight years and ..."

Butler shook his head and walked away from him. I remained behind with the security man for a final look around the bathroom. "Two or three more hours won't matter that much. We'll use that time to try another approach."

His eyes were steady and level on me. "I don't understand how you fit into this."

"I don't either," I said.

"Who does Anna know in Atlanta?"

Butler was driving to my house. I hunched over in the passenger seat and rubbed the scar in the palm of my right hand. As much as I rubbed the scar, it wouldn't go away. "Busco."

"He left town."

"Did he?"

"Anybody else?"

"She knows me."

Butler shook his head. "Anybody else?"

"Not that I know of."

"Busco. You think he might still be in town?"

"It's a big city," I said.

"How would you find him, if he's in a hole somewhere?"

"Drugs. That's his business."

"I'll need Hump," I said.

Butler nodded. "Use him."

I closed my eyes and tried to find a handle. This way or that way or a little bit of both. What I needed was contact with a small-time dealer who had known ties to Busco. A petty dealer who wouldn't keep much inventory. Bait him and watch him run to ...

Butler braked. I opened my eyes. We were parked in front of my house, behind Anna's blue BMW.

"I'll need some bait money. At least two thousand. I know it's a bad day, the banks closed and all, but ..."

"No problem." Frank took the keys from the ignition and leaned across me to unlock the glove compartment. What he had inside looked like a thick sheaf of road maps. He fingered the stack and brought out a brown, legal-sized envelope. He split a nub of scotch tape and opened the envelope. He counted twenty hundreds into my hand. "That enough?"

"You'll get it back unless I'm mugged."

"Do your best." He jammed the envelope into the sheaf of maps and closed the glove compartment and locked it. "Call me at the unlisted home number."

I said I would. I folded the hundreds and stuffed them in my hip pocket and buttoned the pocket. I watched him drive away.

Charles had constructed himself a camp in front of the television set. The second half of the game had just started. He'd found the bread, the mayo and the cold cuts. I stopped long enough to slap a couple of slices of lunchmeat on a piece of bread. I chewed that while I got the zipper case that I carried the .38 belly gun in from the closet in the bedroom. I dropped the case on the bed, chewed and swallowed and dialed Hump's number.

"You busy?" I asked.

"Picking the wax from my ears. If you call that busy."

"I need a name. A small-time dealer a person could buy coke from."

"You a coke head now or are you planning a party?"

"Neither. The dealer has got to be somebody who's small potatoes. And he's got to be one who used to deal with Busco. I need a name and a place."

"You don't want much, do you?"

"If it's impossible, say so."

"Give me ten minutes, Jim."

I said I was at home and broke the connection. I pulled the jack on the phone and carried it into the living room. I plugged it in and placed a pen and paper on the table beside it. I got a Bud from the kitchen and stood behind Charles. "How's the game?"

"Some team I don't care about playing another team I don't care about."

It seemed to be a good critique of what the Game of the Week usually was. I watched it long enough to see that it was Iowa playing Missouri. For all the interest I had it could have been the University of Mars against Moon U.

The phone rang. It was Hump. "I've got a likely one."

I wrote it down. *Beaky Collins. Hector's.* "You feel like coming along?"

It was my way of asking for help.

"What do you have in mind?"

It was his way of saying yes.

I told Hump to meet me across the street from Hector's in twenty minutes.

He said he'd be there.

I parked behind Hector's Club. I crossed the street, dodging the heavy traffic on West Peachtree, and ran up to Hump's '76 Buick and got inside. He was sitting in the driver's seat, sipping a warm beer. I told him what I wanted to try.

"It's probably a waste of time," he said. "The chances are one in a hundred. Less than that. Maybe one in a thousand."

"You got a better way?"

He didn't.

"Stay awake." I left him and crossed West Peachtree again and entered Hector's Club. The bar was dark and crowded with the afternoon trade. There was a larger room with tables through an entranceway to the left. In the evening, there were go-go girls and wet t-shirt night in there.

There was a color TV over the bar. The same game, Iowa and Missouri, was in the last minutes of the fourth quarter. I had the feeling nobody at the bar was especially interested in that game. What they wanted, I decided, were updated scores on the regional games.

A bartender and a barmaid split the duty. With all the customers seated at the bar, the barmaid didn't have much to do. She pressed a serving tray to her flat chest and tried to "work" the bar for any profit she could. I heard one of the men call her Billie. I studied her. She was thin and blonde and looked mistreated. There was a black bruise the size of a man's hand on her right thigh. Net stockings didn't hide the discoloration.

I sipped a scotch and watched her. I heard her ask a couple of men if they wanted to buy bootleg tapes. One man tried to get rid of her by saying that he didn't own a tape player. Billie said, "I'll sell you one, still in the box." When he shook his head, she grinned and said, "Well, maybe you want to buy a box."

One of the customers laughed and said, "Not if you're still giving it away."

I stared at her long enough for her to realize I was interested. Then I looked away. It took her only a couple of minutes to reach my end of the bar. "I don't think I've seen you here before." She stopped on my left and leaned against the back of my bar chair.

"Two or three times," I said. "I remember you." It was a lie that seemed to brighten her afternoon. "You want a drink?"

"I like champagne."

"A real drink," I said. "I'm not a tourist."

"Rob." Billie lifted a hand to the bartender. "Pour me a Remy Martin."

Rob poured. I pushed my cash toward the back of the bar and let him help himself.

"Bottoms up." Billie threw back her head and tossed the cognac down in one swallow.

"That's an interesting idea." I laughed. Billie laughed with me. "Another?"

She nodded. I waved a finger at her empty glass and Rob poured again. This time Billie placed the drink in front of her and turned the glass slowly in her hand. "You trying to get me drunk, stranger?"

I shook my head. "I'm looking for some goodwill. I heard maybe I could get in touch with Beaky Collins here."

"I think he's out of town this weekend."

"Too bad." I sniffed slightly and smiled. "I'm having a party tonight. I've got everything I need to make it a good party except the dessert."

"You a cop?"

"Me?" I shook my head. "You know what a lobbyist is?"

"Somebody hangs around lobbies?"

"Close." I laughed with her. Then I explained the job, keeping it as simple as I could.

"I could make a call. I can't promise anything."

I peeled a twenty from a roll and passed it to her. "Phone change," I said.

She smiled and tucked the twenty in her bra. "Back in a second," she said to the bartender. I watched her enter the large room where the stage was. A turn and she was out of sight. I ordered another scotch.

Billie returned a couple of minutes later. She lifted her cognac and looked over the rim of the glass. "He'll be right here."

"Who?"

"Beaky."

"Thanks a lot, Billie." I toasted her with my drink.

"You better not be a cop."

I assured her that I wasn't.

I knew Beaky Collins had arrived when Billie touched my arm and said, "Wait here." She left me and met a man who'd entered and stood a step inside the front door. Billie talked to him for a few seconds. He lifted his eyes and looked past her shoulder. He was a sport. That was obvious. He wore a well-tailored, blue-black blazer and gray slacks and Gucci loafers. His shirt was open-necked so the gold chains showed and a pinkie ring glittered on his right hand. There was a hook to his nose and I made my guess that was where he'd got his nickname.

Billie introduced him to me. He perched on a chair on my right and we made some small talk. I offered him a drink but he said it was early for him. Billie patted my shoulder and moved away.

Talk of my business. Talk of where I lived. He even asked for a look at my driver's license. I passed the wallet to him. He studied the photo on the license and nodded. "Let's get a breath of air."

I pushed a couple of ones toward the back of the bar for Rob and followed Beaky. On the way out, I waved at Billie and she smiled. Outside the entrance to the bar, I was careful not to look across West Peachtree. I hoped to hell that Hump was awake. We walked around to the rear of Hector's. There were a dozen or so cars in the lot there. Beaky stopped and turned slowly. A look at each car. He took a couple of steps and stopped. "You drop something?"

There was a packet at my feet. I bent down and palmed it.

"Looks like a gram," Beaky said.

"What's the finder's fee?"

"One."

I unbuttoned my hip pocket and passed him the top hundred from the fold. His eyes estimated the fold. Then he lowered his eyes and moved in the direction of a white Corvette. I followed him to the driver's side.

"You know my business?"

"Billie said you lobbied."

"In my business, I could use a bigger buy. An ounce."

"You got the cash?"

I spread the fold of hundreds.

"I don't have that much on hand," he said.

"Maybe you could tell me who does."

"I didn't say I couldn't get it." The greed was on him. "Twenty-four hundred?"

"Two thousand," I said.

"Split the difference," Beaky said. "Twenty-two."

"If it's the good stuff."

"It will be." He opened the door to the Corvette. "It might take an hour. Where'll you be?"

"At home." I found a scrap of paper in my packet and wrote down my phone number. "Call me."

He drove away. I got into my car and waited a couple of minutes. When I pull onto West Peachtree, I looked across the street. Hump's '76 Buick was gone. He hadn't been asleep after all.

CHAPTER TEN

Charles was asleep on the couch when I got home. I closed the door. I placed the phone beside my bed and stretched out on it, fully clothed except for my shoes. I closed my eyes but I couldn't sleep.

An hour dragged past.

The phone rang. It was Frank Butler. "What the hell is going on, Jim?"

"I'm waiting for a call. Let me call you back. I want the phone clear."

Fifteen minutes. Twenty minutes. The phone rang. I heard movement in the living room. Charles was awake and stirring about.

It was Hump this time.

"Yeah, Hump?"

"It's Busco you want, right?"

I said it was.

"I'm not sure about Busco, but I've seen one of his boys."

"Where?"

Hump had followed Beaky Collins across half of the city. The first two stops Collins made he was out of luck. Nobody home at a place on Claremont, The same at a house on Pine Street. The third stop was the charm. Hump followed Collins to an apartment complex in Buckhead. The Spanish Main Apartments.

"You know where it is?"

I said I had a fairly good idea.

Hump almost lost Beaky there. He'd been laying back too far on the tail. Lost him but circled back and drove through the complex until he spotted the white Corvette. That was in Section D of the complex. Hump pulled in and parked several cars down the row from the Corvette. Beaky came out after about ten minutes. The big man who worked for Busco was with him.

"Herb," I said.

Beaky was carrying a mailing envelope in one hand. He talked for a minute or two with the big man and then he got into his Corvette and drove away. The big man returned to the apartment.

"You get a number for the apartment?"

"I wasn't sure at first." Hump was thinking of leaving his car and going into the hallway for a look at the names on the mailboxes. That was risky. Busco's man knew him. The way it turned out, he didn't have to leave the car. The drapes opened at the window of the ground level apartment to the right of the entranceway to Section D. Hump saw the big man at the window.

"Anything else?"

"I wanted to give you an apartment number. I drove over to another part of the complex. In Section A the ground floor apartment to the right of the entranceway is marked A2. I'd say, unless there's some reason for a change, Busco's man was in D2."

"That's it, Hump. You can go. I owe you one."

"Since when did we start keeping score?" He sounded offended. He hung up before I could apologize.

I dialed Butler's home number. He listened for a couple of minutes as I talked then he said: "You think Busco's there?"

"Maybe."

"And Anna?"

"Could be."

"I've got to make a few calls. I'll be by for you as soon as I can."

"What?"

"Wait there."

I unplugged the phone. If I left it on, I might have to buy that ounce of cocaine. Tough on Beaky Collins. Screw him. Maybe it would be hard on Billie. That was what she got for trusting strangers.

Born losers both of them. I knew a loser when I saw one. All I had to do was look in the mirror.

Charles stumbled in from the living room. He yawned and rubbed his eyes. "You find Miss Anna?"

"We'll know soon."

"I hope ..."

"What do you know about drugs, Charles?"

"This between you and me?"

I nodded.

"I smoke some. Started in high school."

"What do you know about Anna and drugs?"

"Me?" He acted shocked.

"You," I insisted.

"I seen her snort a couple of times. At the Farm before I drove her to town last Sunday and one time up at the hotel later."

"You buy for her, Charles?"

"Aw, Mr. Hardman." He ducked his head. "One time. That Sunday. She didn't want to leave the baby. She made a call and she gave me five, hundred-dollar bills. She told me to walk to Central City Park. I was to look for a man wearing a blue wind-breaker and carrying a rolled-up umbrella. I walked down there. I met the man and he asked me if I was Anna's nigger. I had to say that I was. I gave him the money and he gave me the envelope."

"A man with a hook in his nose?"

He nodded.

"Don't worry about it," I said. "Nothing else you could do when Anna asked you."

"Not after how she's been with my grandma."

Time passed slowly, Charles yawned a few more times and returned to the couch. I heard the coach squeak under his weight and then there was quiet.

By my watch it was an hour since I'd called Frank Butler. Then an hour and fifteen minutes. I paced my bedroom. The sky grew dark. It looked like it might rain.

I was on the bed, head back, eyes closed, when I heard tires squeal on the street in front of the house. I heard two car doors slam. I went to the front door, half expecting to find Beaky Collins there. Instead I found Frank Butler and a heavyset man with gray hair and a thick gray mustache. Butler introduced me to William Turnbull of the D.E.A. "William wants one more shot at Busco."

"I hope he's there."

"But you know one of Busco's men is at the apartment?"

"One hundred percent." If Hump didn't recognize a man who'd worked him over I was in trouble. I didn't think I was.

"We go now?" Turnbull said.

He led the way. I was one step behind with Frank. "Police narcotics has the place staked out until we get there with the warrant."

I stopped on the sidewalk. "You need me?"

Butler nodded. "You can recognize Busco's man."

That was true.

Turnbull's driver pulled around the side of Section D of the Spanish Main Apartments and parked next to a dust-covered VW van. The van was the stake-out car. As soon as Turnbull's car braked, a man in jeans, a denim shirt and a fringed buckskin jacket trotted from the van over to us. Turnbull rolled down the window on his side of the car.

"You might have taken too long getting the warrant," the man in the buckskin jacket said.

"How's that?"

"Two men left the apartment carrying suitcases. That was forty minutes ago."

"Busco one of them?"

"Neither man matched the picture."

"You didn't stop them?" Turnbull showed the man a stern face.

"No way I could."

"Describe the men."

"One was big, like a wrestler. The other one smaller. They left in an Impala."

"Where are they now?"

"We had a man follow them. They're at Hartsfield now. They've made stops at most of the ticket windows. They're looking for a flight to New York."

"They find a flight?"

The man nodded. "Boarding in fifteen minutes."

Turnbull opened the car door and stepped out. Butler followed. I stretched and yawned and joined them. "Let's try it here and see what we've got," Turnbull said.

The narcotics cop in the buckskin jacket knocked on the door to D2. I leaned past him and put an ear to the door. I could hear music. I touched my ear and backed away. The cop raised an eyebrow at me and then pressed his ear against the door. He nodded and mouthed, "I hear it."

He knocked again.

William Turnbull was impatient. "Break it in."

The cop in the buckskin jacket pivoted and nodded at the two men who'd followed us from the van. One of them, stepping around me, reached under his soiled raincoat and brought out what looked like a five-pound hammer on a sawed-off handle. He swung the hammer against the door in the space between the knob and the frame. Once, twice and the lock broke and the wood splintered. The lock clattered to the floor inside the apartment. The man with the hammer backed away. The other one rammed his shoulder against the door and pushed. It gave and swung inward.

The room we were in was stifling hot. The hot air rushed past us. On that rush of air was a rotten, sickening smell. It was the smell of guts.

I gagged and caught myself.

It was there on the white carpet. The body of a man in blue undershorts. He was naked otherwise. The narc cop in the buckskin jacket leaned over the mm. "Busco," he said.

Butler said, "What the hell...?" I stepped around him and had a brief look. It was Busco all right, He was on his back. What looked to be about a six-inch slicing knife was planted in his chest, just below the sternum. There was another deep slash in Busco's stomach. That was where the gut rot smell came from.

"Stone cold dead," the narc cop said.

I swallowed hard and stepped around the body. That was when I heard the sound. It was part moan and part whine. I could hear it just above the music that came from the tape player. There was a door straight ahead and it was slightly ajar. I went in that direction. When I reached the door, I gave it a gentle push and stepped aside.

Anna Gault sat cross-legged on the bed. Her legs were folded under her in what looked to be a yoga position. She was dressed in a white nightgown that was stained all down the front with dried blood. Her hands, loose in her lap and palms up, were stained with blood as well.

"Anna."

She didn't react. I stepped to the foot of the bed, close enough to look at her eyes. She didn't blink. Her eyes were glazed over, hooded as if against a strong light.

I returned to the doorway. "Frank. In here."

He pushed past me. I heard a hiss from him that sounded like "shit". If I hadn't been so shocked by Anna's condition, I might have reacted to Butler's language. It was, if I'd heard him correctly, the first time I'd heard him say shit.

Turnbull stopped in the doorway behind me. "Is she hurt?"

"I think she's in shock," I said.

"Get her out of here, Jim," Butler said. "Take her to your place."

I looked at Turnbull. He nodded.

There was a folded blanket on a chair beside the bed. I shook it open and wrapped it around her. When I lifted her, she clutched at me and said, "Carl ... Carl ..." Butler stepped forward and lifted the trailing end of the blanket and tucked it under Anna's legs.

Turnbull's driver opened the back door to the black Mercedes. I got in still carrying Anna. She was heavy, dead weight. Turnbull walked aside a couple of paces and took the driver with him. A few words and the driver returned and started the car's engine.

"He said to take you home."

I gave him the address.

I called the security man at the Peachtree Plaza. With some prompting, he remembered me and that I'd been with Frank Butler. I told him I'd be sending Mrs. Gault's driver Charles over to pick up her things. I asked if he could have one of the maids do the packing before he got there. He said he'd see to it.

Water ran in the tub. I adjusted the mix until the temperature felt right. I closed the taps and returned to the living room. Charles stood beside the sofa, staring down at Anna. I peeled the blanket away and lifted Anna and carried her into the bathroom. "Charles, I need you in here."

He hesitated in the doorway. I could see that he was embarrassed. "Mr. Hardman, I don't think I ought to ..."

I didn't have time to deal with his modesty. "Hold her upright," I said.

He caught her under the arms. I pulled the nightgown that far. He blinked and his eyes closed tight before he lowered his hands and caught her by the waist. I tugged the gown over her head and dropped it on the toilet seat. I lifted her and placed her, as gently as I could, into the bath water. For an irrational moment, I almost wished I had some kid's bubble bath. I didn't. I found a wash cloth and began scrubbing the bad patches of blood from her. When I looked around, Charles had left the bathroom.

I left Anna to soak. I braced her head against the end of the tub so she wouldn't fall forward. I found Charles in the living room. I took a twenty from my pocket and passed it to him. "That's for the maid who's packing Mrs. Gault's things."

"Yes, sir." His eyes wouldn't meet mine.

I wrote down Frank Butler's law firm and the address. "When you see the security man at the Plaza, give him this. Tell him to bill Mr. Butler for whatever charges Mrs. Gault has at the hotel."

He left. I returned to the bathroom and used some of my shampoo to wash Anna's hair. When I was sure she was clean, I drained the tub and wrapped her in several towels, I carried her into my bedroom. My bathrobe smelled of tobacco and sweat and me but I didn't have any choice. I got her into the robe, belted it and covered her with a sheet and a blanket.

Her eyes fluttered a time or two but there was no recognition of me in them.

The hotel maid's packing was neat and careful. I found underwear in one of the large suitcases and her robe in the other. Charles remained steadfast in the kitchen while I stripped her and struggled to slip underpants on her. That done, I had to tilt her forward to hook a bra on her. The robe was next. I got one arm in and had to roll her this way and that to put the other arm through.

I'd finished buttoning the robe when I heard Frank's voice in the living room. I covered Anna with a sheet and blanket went into the kitchen, where Butler, with Charles' help, had found my booze. Frank was slugging down a double shot of my medium good scotch, one hip braced against the kitchen counter, when I entered. "How is she?"

"I gave her a bath."

"Besides that?"

"Still not in this world," I said. I found a glass and poured myself a neat scotch.

"Police picked up Busco's two men at the airport. It was close. They were in line, about to board an Eastern flight to New York."

I nodded.

"They say Anna killed Busco. According to them, Anna and their boss had a knockdown fight because he was leaving Atlanta and heading north and didn't want to take her and the baby along."

"What did you expect them to say?"

Butler considered it a moment. "One of the suitcases they had with them was almost full of cash. The last I heard the police were still counting it."

"Money's a good reason for killing."

"One reason," Butler said. He didn't sound at all sure it was the only possible reason.

I sat at the kitchen table and closed my eyes. I tried to rub the ache away. "I think I've been dipped in this shit enough times."

"All right."

"I think I'm five years ahead on my Boy Scout good deeds."

"I owe you," Butler said. "Call the I.O.U. the next time you need it."

I felt rough. "I bet you don't think I will."

"I know you. You will."

The ambulance arrived a few minutes later while Butler and I were trying to decide whether we had anything more to say to each other. Anna left strapped on a stretcher, Butler going with her, and was taken to Grady Hospital. She was admitted to the psychiatric wing there. It was several days before she was well enough to talk to police about what had happened at the Spanish Main Apartments. Butler told me later that she said all she remembered was going into the living room and finding Carl Busco on the carpet, dying. She'd tried to help him and that was how she got covered with his blood. After that she didn't remember anything until she regained consciousness at Grady.

The railroad tracks ran straight through the front door of the Fulton County Courthouse and out the back wall. Herbert Sizemore and Paul Grafton, who'd worked for the late Carl Busco, had about the chance of a wet cat in a microwave oven. None at all.

I sat through most of the trial. The D.A.'s man argued that Sizemore and Grafton had killed Carl Busco for the grand sum of two hundred and twenty-four thousand dollars and some change. They'd been apprehended trying to leave the state with a suitcase of money. Traces of Busco's blood had been found on the clothing of both men and on their shoes. The only other witness to that murder was in a private institution recovering from drug abuse and emotional shock. On the advice of her doctor, she could not be called to testify.

It was not the most airtight case I'd ever heard. In fact, as a former cop, I thought it leaked and clanked. The defense lawyer, a public defender appointed by the court, must have known how the wind was blowing. On the second morning, he threw in the towel. He plea bargained it down to manslaughter and that got Sizemore and Grafton seven-to-ten. I passed the public defender in the hall granting an interview to a newspaper reporter. From the way he talked, he'd won a great victory.

What he'd really done was step out of the path of the freight train. A life sentence or death, that was what he'd avoided.

In early December, I drove to Gaultsville again.

It was cold, crisp weather. The trees were bare and the land I passed through was barren and hooded over by a layer of frost.

The call had come from Charles on a Saturday morning. Mr. Gault wanted to see me and he asked me to pick a time when I could visit. I checked my schedule. It was blank. I got in my car and started driving.

It was a few minutes before noon when I parked the car in front of the mansion. At the front door, a neat black girl in a nurse's uniform met me and led me through the house and to the office where I'd had my other talk with Harrison Gault.

He was waiting for me, prepared as if I'd entered a stage set. The drapes at the wide window were open. There was a bright slant of winter light through the glass. Gault wore dark glasses and his chair was turned so that he could look out at the corral. The corral was empty now.

"Fix yourself a drink, Mr. Hardman." Gault indicated a silver ice bucket on his desk one glass and a bottle of the Clynelesh.

I studied the label on the single malt scotch. It was from the same shipment that I'd received a bottle of after my visit to Gault Farm. The label appeared homemade and the proof and the age of the scotch had been inked in by hand.

I poured and avoided the ice bucket.

"You received your bottle by way of Mr. Butler. I assume."

"Yes, thank you." I took a sip and rolled it around on my tongue. "I'm saving it. I think I'll put it in my stocking for Christmas."

At the far side of the corral, a man opened a gate and led the Morgan stud through it. The man was black and I had to squint against the strong light. It took me a few seconds to realize that the black man dressed in jeans, a denim jacket, a red shirt, cowboy boots and a white Stetson hat was Charles.

The Morgan was saddled. Charles mounted the Morgan with ease and once he was in the saddle he walked the horse slowly around the perimeters of the corral.

"That's Charles, isn't it?" I knew it was. I wanted to hear what Harrison Gault would say.

"Yes. He's learning to ride. Did you know there were many black cowboys in the Old West?"

"I've read that somewhere."

"Superb horsemen by all accounts."

"Charles rides well?"

"He'll get better with the practice."

Charles circled the corral three times. After the final circuit, he pulled at the reins and moved the Morgan into the center of the corral. The Morgan stopped. Charles lifted the white Stetson from his head, swept it downward and bowed. He remained that way for a count of ten. He straightened and pulled at the reins. The hat still held low, Charles trotted the Morgan toward the gate. When he reached it, he dismounted and led the stud through the gate and out of sight beyond the corner of the house.

Harrison Gault smiled.

I tapped the palms of my hands together in polite applause.

"Yes, wasn't it?" Gault said.

"I'm impressed."

"I have something I want you to read." Now Gault was all business. His voice had changed. "There. On the center of the desk."

I found a letter there. I carried it to the window where the light was better. It began: *Dear Mrs. Anna Gault.*

I lowered the letter and looked at Gault.

"It came here," he said. "It was, of course, addressed to Anna. On Butler's advice I opened it. In Anna's condition, the state she's in at the institution, I couldn't very well forward a letter to her that might upset her and spoil the progress of the treatment she is receiving."

It was a good argument. Advice of the lawyer was a good touch as well.

Recently I had occasion to treat a female prisoner at the Wickwire Detention Center for Women. Her condition is quite serious, the result of a rare blood disease. Her reaction to treatment has not been favorable to this point.

The prisoner-patient confided to me that her crime, for which she is at present serving a ten-year sentence, was a shared crime. She insists that she took full blame for a murder which she committed in partnership with another person. The person she named as co-criminal is you, Mrs. Gault.

I have no way to judge the truth of her statement. The young girl is distraught and told me that she has not heard from you for a period of months. Whatever the truth or falsehood of her charges I do, however, believe that it would be a Christian kindness if you would resume your correspondance with the prisoner-patient. It might make her last days or weeks happier ones.

She asked to be remembered to you as Mitka.

The letter was signed *Evan Turner-Ross, Prison Surgeon.*

I returned the letter to the desk and placed it where it had been. I stopped next to the Clynelesh and poured myself a strong drink. "It's vague."

"You met this girl … whatever her name is."

"Mitka."

"You believe the letter?"

I hesitated. "I believe the letter was written. I believe that a prison surgeon thought enough of Mitka's story and her condition to write Anna. Beyond that, I don't know what it is that I am supposed to believe or not believe. How long has Anna been in the institution?"

"Something over a month."

"Then it is unlikely, in such a short time, that Anna's inability to write Mitka would have brought on such an angry reaction."

"You're skirting the question. What do you really believe?"

"I don't know. Look at it this way. They were close friends. Anna got what Mitka wanted. That was your grandson, Harry. Later, like some fairy tale, Anna ended up over here. She's living the good life while Mitka is doing time. Add to that the fact that Mitka is ill. Dying even. The story Mitka told the doctor might be a kind of revenge against the circumstances. Anna got everything. She got nothing." Suddenly I had a thought. It wasn't one I liked. "You're not going to ask me to fly to London again, are you?"

"No reason to," Gault said. "I called the doctor three days ago. The girl died a couple of days after the doctor wrote the letter. It seems to have been some kind of rare blood cancer and it was hopeless."

I drained my glass. I didn't want another drink. The day was darker now than it had been when I left Atlanta. "I'm sorry about the girl. It seems unfair. The lives going off in different directions the way they did. What gives me a doubt about Mitka's story is that I was there when she confessed. I didn't see any pressure from Anna on her. Mitka confessed that she killed Harry, that she buried him. Nowhere was there a suggestion or a hint that Anna was involved at all."

He sighed. "I think that is why I needed to talk to you. You've eased my mind, Mr. Hardman."

"One day, when Anna is well, I think we ought to show her the letter and see what she has to say."

"Vague charges from someone who is dead? That is not fair either."

"Perhaps you're right." I placed the glass on the tray with the ice bucket and said goodbye.

❖ ❖ ❖

When I got to my car, I found Charles in the front passenger seat. The window on that side was cracked a couple of inches. An acrid smoke was drawn through that opening. I passed that side of the car and sniffed. It was weed.

I rounded the hood of the car and opened the door and got behind the wheel. Charles still wore the jeans and the denim jacket. He'd exchanged the red fancy shirt for a gray work shirt. I didn't see the white Stetson and he wore brogans rather than the cowboy boots.

"Wild west," I said. "When you going on the rodeo circuit?"

He lowered his head and shook it slowly from side to side. "I feel like such a damned fool when he has me do that."

"It looked staged."

"Took him a week to work it out the way he wants it. Now he has me do it every time he has a visitor."

I started the engine. He didn't move. "You going any place in particular?"

"I thought you might give me a lift into Gaultsville. It's Saturday and you know how niggers are about Saturday nights."

Using *nigger* was an indication how he felt about himself. A southern black might call another black a nigger, and he might use the word in front of another black. But he wouldn't refer to himself that way unless he was turning some anger inward, back against himself. Not in front of a white.

We left Gault Farm behind. I took the turn that pointed us toward the short main street of Gaultsville. When he didn't tell me where he wanted to be dropped off, I waited and waited and then parked outside the final building on Main Street. Wellum's Tavern. "Which juke joint you spending the day in?"

"I got a choice of four." He hooked a thumb at Wellum's Tavern. "This ain't one of them."

I'd been thinking about the performance in the corral outside old Gault's window. "You don't have to stay here in Gaultsville. If you come to Atlanta, I'll help you get settled and help you find work."

"It ain't that easy. I got family here."

"The offer's good until spring." I grinned at him. "What I wanted to ask you was how Miss Anna is."

"Frank Butler tells me she's better."

Charles opened the door on his side of the car. "That old man back there is crazy."

"Anna might be crazy too."

Charles slid across the seat. His feet touched the street. He stood and turned back to me. "It might be that you and me are the only ones ain't crazy. You think about it." He closed the car door and turned away.

I watched him walk half a block or so, back the way we'd come. He turned and entered an alley or a narrow side street and was gone.

I reached Atlanta early that afternoon. I had a few beers at George's Deli. It was getting early dark when I left there and went by the Superior to buy some groceries and a case of beer.

As soon as I entered my house the phone was ringing. It was Hump.

"What you doing tonight, Jim?"

I said that I was thinking about watching some TV or finding a movie I wanted to see.

"That white stuff you said you bought … you still got it?"

The packet of cocaine that I'd bought from Beaky Collins in the parking lot behind Hector's Bar. The gram. "Yeah."

"That's good news. A girl I know has a sister visiting her from out of town. I think she wants to try out her nose."

"Just the sister?"

"All our noses," Hump said.

"Where do I fit in?"

"The sister."

"Have you seen her, Hump?"

"She's a busted bale of hay but she's got a great personality."

"Stop by for the packet. You can do some other friend my favor."

"You open that fancy scotch yet?"

I had it hidden away. "Yeah, but ..."

"Say we drop by around eight-thirty. The sister likes good scotch too."

"Is she really ...?"

"Naw. She's about an eight. I was thinking of trading you Sally even for her."

"What's her name?"

"Prissy," Hump said. "Now, ain't that a name for you?"

I had a bit more than an hour. I wasted half of that doing some cleaning. I'd heard somewhere that a woman judged a man by the way he kept his bathroom. I polished the tub, the wash basin and the toilet and swept the dust from the floor. I changed the sheets and pillowcases in thé bedroom and ran the vacuum cleaner once over lightly on the living room carpet. After I showered and dressed, I cracked the bottle of Clynelesh. I poured myself the virgin shot of it.

Prissy was from Columbia, South Carolina and she felt wicked and sinful in the big city.

We drank my good scotch and the three of them snorted the gram of cocaine. I said I'd had some before they arrived, that I hadn't been able to wait for them.

Sunday morning the whole house smelled of ribs and sauce. We'd ordered from a takeout place and made pigs of ourselves. Prissy was in my bed looking swollen-eyed and used and I could hear animal grunting from the living room where Hump and Sally were.

I had a couple of Alka-Seltzers and returned to bed. My weight in the bed disturbed Prissy. She rolled toward me and stared at me through slit eyes. There was a dazed look on her face. "Who are you?"

"The snowman," I said.

"Oh, yes," she murmured, "I remember you." She grabbed my shoulders and pulled me against her. Her armpits smelled like a wet mule. But, I thought as I lowered my hands and rubbed the curves of her ass, this is what a Saturday night is supposed to be, isn't it?

CHAPTER ELEVEN

I awoke early on Monday morning. It was a spun sugar world outside. Everything coated with ice. The grass, the ground and all the trees. Some of the smaller trees bent under the weight of layers and crusts of ice.

The house was a mess from my little party. I made coffee. I had to wait for the water to settle through the grounds. While that was happening, I had juice and an apple and a wedge of cheddar cheese. I'd read somewhere that an apple and cheese are a good, healthy breakfast. The truth was it didn't taste all that pleasant early in the morning. I put bread in the toaster and got whipped butter and a jar of blueberry preserves from the refrigerator.

The coffee was ready. I carried a cup of it and a plate of buttered toast and a glop of preserves into the living room. I chewed at the toast and, just for the hell of it, I opened the curtains at the front of the house and peered out. It was the same as it was from the bedroom window. Only a different view. The leaves and the lawn were coated with ice and the walk was slick and glistening.

I blinked. An ambulance was parked at the curb. The engine was running. Exhaust ribboned from the pipe and the windows of the wagon were fogged so I couldn't see who was inside. I guessed it was Anna.

It took me a couple of minutes to get down the iced-over stairs. I avoided the walkway and crept along on the lawn. There was more traction and give there. It was noisy going. Ice crunched under my shoes. Leaves cracked.

I'd hardly reached the sidewalk when the door on the curb side of the ambulance opened and Anna smiled at me. She reached behind her and switched off the engine.

"I thought you'd never awaken, Miami."

"How long have you been out here?"

"An hour."

I thought she was lying. The windshield was completely iced over. The street under the car was hardly iced at all. Still, to be fair, she could be telling the truth. The heat of the engine could have melted the frozen sheet beneath the car. Maybe. Maybe not. But she was definitely crazy.

"Come in and have a cup of coffee," I said. I hoped if I was calm, she'd be calm.

She wore an expensive white trench coat. Cowboy boots with her Calvin Klein jeans stuffed in the tops and a heavy white fisherman's knit sweater. While she removed her coat and looked around the living room, I got her a cup of coffee. I watched color return to her face, either from the heat of the room or the hot coffee.

"You have any trouble finding me, Anna?"

She smiled. "I found your home months and months ago. I hoped you would invite me here." She pouted. "You never did."

"I guess things weren't going well for you at the hospital."

"I don't feel safe there," she said. "I feel safe with you."

I followed Anna into the kitchen and stood back while she opened the refrigerator and looked inside. She found a bunch of white grapes and rinsed them at the sink. Her back was to me while she ate about half of the grapes. When she turned and faced me there was a misting of tears in her eyes.

"You'd be better off at the Farm."

"I don't like it there."

"Little Harry is there. Wouldn't you like to see him?" I asked.

She nodded. "You'd better call Mr. Gault."

"I can't," she said. "Perhaps you would call for me."

One more time. I'd made a vow to myself never to get involved with her problems again. *Never again.* Now, one more time. This time and it would be over for good. I wanted to believe that. Against all my better judgment.

I went into the bedroom. I placed the call to Gault Farm. A woman answered.

I gave her my name. "Is Mr. Gault available?"

"I'll see," she said.

There was a long wait before he came on the line. His voice was weak and reedy. "Yes, Mr. Hardman?"

"Anna's here. She took an ambulance."

"I thought she might show up there."

"You want me to send her home?"

"Could you bring her? I'm not sure I'd trust her to drive back here by herself."

"Send Charles for her."

"Him? I wouldn't trust him as far as I can spit. She can wrap him around her finger any time she wants to."

"I'd rather not."

"How about if I hire somebody to make the drive?"

"You know anybody you can trust not to get conned by Anna? What if she's halfway here and decides she really wants to be in New York?"

He had a good point. "All right. But we make a deal. After this, I burn your phone number and you burn mine."

Harrison Gault laughed. "I'll have your phone number buried with me. That all right with you?"

"A deal."

"When can we expect you?"

"Later in the day. I want to see if some of this ice melts."

"Ice?"

"Big ice storm here in Atlanta," I said.

"Come as soon as you're sure it's safe."

I said I would and broke the connection. I entered the living room and switched on the TV set. I flipped channels until I found a local morning show that usually carried weather reports. I had to listen to a lot of talky crap about what to do with leftovers and Mr. Fix-It told me how to replace a window pane. I was about to give up when the weatherman came on. The ice storm, I learned, was isolated, confined to the city and the suburbs. I cut the TV off.

Anna stood just behind me. "What did he say?"

"He asked me to drive you to Gaultsville."

"Will you?"

"It looks like I'm elected."

"When?"

"Later. When some of the ice has melted."

"Then I will use your shower,"

"Help yourself," I said. I passed her and went into the kitchen. I dumped the cold coffee and refilled my cup. I braced a hip against the sink and stared through the window. Like that, I heard the first drip, drip. The ice in the sun was beginning to melt.

I heard the shower running. I entered the living room and glanced toward the bath room. The door was open and Anna stood there, naked, facing me.

"I don't have a robe," Anna said.

I took a couple of steps toward her. She lifted her arms from her sides as if she waited for me to step through the doorway and grab her. I reached the doorway and stopped. I leaned forward and caught the doorknob. I pulled the door closed.

There was a short silence on the other side of the door. Then I heard her laughter above the roar of the shower.

It was early afternoon before I was sure the road was safe enough for the drive to Gaultsville. I drove her in my car. Somebody from the hospital was coming for their ambulance. I was sure that Frank Butler would see to it that she was never charged for stealing it.

We drove half the distance in the stony silence that followed the incident in the bathroom. Anna curled up on the far side of the front seat with her back to me. It made it easier for me and I was disturbed when she turned and faced me.

"You don't want me anymore, Miami?"

I didn't look toward her. I had to keep my eyes on the highway. There were patches of ice where the road was shaded.

"Do I repulse you?" she prodded.

"I don't want to get more involved with you, Anna. Your life is a mess and mine is messy enough as it is."

"We could be a mess together."

I shook my head. "I'm sick of other people's problems becoming mine. I'm done with it."

I surprised myself by saying that. Anna didn't speak to me for the rest of the drive.

It was around half past four when we passed through the town of Gaultsville and made the turn toward Gault Farm.

A young black girl in a nurse's uniform met us in Gault's anteroom. Anna went off to look in on little Harry. She hated me now. That was progress as far as I was concerned.

I found my own way to Gault's office.

There was an ice bucket on the desk, one glass and an unopened bottle of Clynelesh.

The wheelchair that Gault sat in was turned so that his back was to the open drapes, the window and the corral beyond. The corral was empty. The weak winter afternoon light streamed in and lit the crown of Gault's head like a halo.

"Pour for yourself, Jim," he said.

I broke the seal and removed the cap. I poured myself a large shot and avoided the ice bucket. I sipped it neat. Yes, it was the genuine article.

"Your health," I said.

"What little of it there is left." He smiled. "Thank you."

I rolled a second swallow of the scotch around my tongue before I let it ease down my throat. "I want Anna out of my life."

"I suppose we have imposed on your goodwill too much."

"At least a time or two too many," I said.

He gave me a firm nod. "I'll make you a promise. I'll keep her away from you if I have to put her on a leash and hold the leash myself."

"Fair enough." I poured the last swallow of the scotch down.

"And we can remain friends?"

"I'd like that." I lied. I didn't want anything to do with Gault, either. But I did like his booze.

"Pour again." He motioned toward the bottle. "I like to see a man enjoy himself." He watched me pour another generous shot. "You'll stay the night?"

I took my time deciding. The low slant of the sun meant that it wasn't long before dark. It would be colder after dark and the ice that had melted during the day would freeze again. It might be better if I didn't risk a nighttime drive. In fact, I'd considered that possibility and I'd packed a small bag before I left the house. My shaving things, a couple of changes of underwear, shirts and socks.

"Thank you. I'll stay the night and make an early start in the morning."

"Good. I'm pleased to have your company."

I realized I hadn't seen Charles when I arrived. "Where's Charles?"

"He is no longer employed by me. I fired him this morning."

"That was sudden, wasn't it?"

"He was insolent to me," Gault said.

"So am I," I said. "I wish you'd fired me."

Dinner was a fresh ham basted in a few cups of dry white wine. That and sweet potatoes and green peas and a tossed salad. And biscuits as light and fluffy as whipped cream.

It was not a comfortable meal. Whatever love Gault had felt for Anna had probably soured by now. Her feelings for me certainly had.

I settled back to endure the meal and stoke my mouth and drink as much of the very good Graves that was served with the ham. Gault and I made some small talk while Anna glowered at me and pushed her food around her plate.

I didn't remain long after the coffee and brandy. I said that I was tired from the drive and I wanted to get to bed early so I could make a seven o'clock start back in the morning.

I did go to sleep early.

But I awoke after what seemed no time at all. I rolled from side-to-side. No use. I was wide awake. I fumbled for the lamp beside the bed.

It was 12:34 by my watch.

I sat on the side of the bed and rubbed the cords on the back of my neck. Better. Not good enough. I remembered that there was an Alka-Seltzer in my shaving kit. I was in the bathroom, rummaging about for the foil wrapped pack, when I heard the footsteps. They were coming from the direction of the staircase that led upward from the first floor. Light feet, I thought. Or on tiptoes.

Coming from the wrong direction. Not what I'd been fearing all night, the visit from the rear wing where Anna's suite of rooms was.

The footsteps slowed. There was a beat, a hesitation, outside my bed room door. Then whoever it was continued until I couldn't hear the footfall anymore.

I found the Alka-Seltzer and drank down the fizz. I belched on my way back to bed. Sometimes the aspirin helped to relax me. Other times it didn't. I switched off the lamp and closed my eyes. In a matter of a few minutes, I was in a deep sleep again.

The knocking at the door was loud, insistent.

A breakfast call? I clawed for the lamp switch and found it. I checked my watch. Until that moment, I thought I'd slept for hours. If my watch was running... I placed it beside my ear and heard the ticking. It was 2:18.

I threw aside the covers and staggered to the door. I opened the door. One of the private security guards stood there with about a foot-long flashlight in his hand.

"You're Hardman, aren't you?"

I said I was.

"My name is Matt Parker. You might not remember me, but I was on duty the night the nurse tried to kill the baby."

I said I remembered him.

"I might need your help. I've called the Sheriff but he's not here yet."

"What is it?"

"There's been an accident. It's Mr. Gault."

I dressed hurriedly and followed him down the staircase. The young black nurse and one of the other house servants huddled together in the anteroom. The house servant was crying. The black nurse tried to comfort her.

"Fix us some coffee," Parker said as we passed. "Make that a big pot. Sheriff Andy Karlin will be here in a few minutes." The guard led me in the direction of old Gault's office. At the last moment, we passed that closed door and turned down a hall. Halfway down that hall, on the right, there was an open door and I looked into a bedroom. "Mr. Gault slept here."

Parker stopped at the closed door at the end of the hallway. There were a series of light switches to the left of the door. He threw one switch and opened the door.

Cold wind blew at us. We were outside. Narrow steps led to the ground level. A wheelchair ramp curled to the left, following the line of the rear of the house. We walked down the ramp. It was slippery with frost. There was a gate at the bottom of the ramp. It was closed now, with the wooden drawbar in place.

The gate led into the corral. It was the corral where I'd seen the Morgan stud, the one where I'd seen Charles do his black cowboy impersonation.

The corral was lighted by a bank of floodlights attached to the roof of the house.

I stopped at the rail. I could feel the beginning of the sickness. I saw the overturned wheelchair first and beyond that the body of the old man. The rail shook under my hands and I looked across the corral and saw the Morgan. The stud slammed himself against the rail and quivered there.

Old Gault had been dressed in trousers, a white undershirt, a dark robe and bedroom slippers. The slipper had fallen from his left foot. The bare whiteness of his skin, the sole of his foot, seemed somehow obscene.

I reached for the drawbar. Parker stirred beside me. His condensed breath blew over my shoulder. "I wouldn't go in there."

"What?"

"Not until Sheriff Karlin gets here."

"What about him?" I waved a hand toward the body of Harrison Gault.

"He's dead. I already checked him."

"You sure?"

"I was a medic in 'Nam."

I stared at the body. Gault was face down on the ground. Both hands were near his head, as if he'd tried to protect himself.

"He's been stomped to a pulp," Parker said.

"When did you find him?"

"Five or ten minutes ago."

"You've been making rounds? When did you first notice the floodlights?"

"The lights weren't on."

I leaned on the rail and lowered my head. "He ever do this before?"

"Do what?"

"Go in the corral by himself late at night."

"Not that I know of," Parker said. "But I couldn't swear in a court he never did. He was a strong-willed man and did anything he wanted to."

A car pulled around the side of the house and stopped on the far side of the corral. A blue light flashed on the roof of the car.

"That's the Sheriff now."

"If the light wasn't on, what made you check the corral?"

He'd walked away a few feet, heading toward the police car. He stopped. "It was that horse. That horse was about to kill himself trying to bust through that fence and get out of the corral."

"The horse usually left in the corral all night?"

"Naw. There's a solid warm barn for him."

I'd asked all my questions. We circled the corral and met Sheriff Karlin and his deputy. Karlin was a lank, tall man with gray hair and a face that didn't seem to have cheekbones. There were sunken places where the bones should have been.

"The doctor and the ambulance are on the way," Karlin said. He walked to the rail fence and looked at the body and then the horse. "Somebody ought to kill that goddam horse," he mumbled.

❧ ❧ ❧

It was a room off to one side of the kitchen. At one time, when the house had first been built, it had probably been a large walk-in pantry and storage room. Now it had been converted into a dining room for the house staff.

The cook placed mugs and cream and sugar on the table. She returned with a twelve-cup percolator. She put the coffee pot on a wire rack and backed away. There were four mugs and only three of us in the dining room. The deputy was still outside waiting for the doctor and the ambulance.

Sheriff Karlin nodded at the security guard and Parker moved to the door and closed it.

"Smells of niggers in here," Karlin said.

I sniffed. I didn't smell anything but the coffee.

Karlin gulped his coffee. "But it's damned good coffee, especially on a morning like this."

"The old man appreciated good coffee," Parker said. "Insisted on it."

"That nigger boy took care of the stud for Mr. Gault ... what's his name?"

"Charles." Parker took a big swallow of coffee and burned his mouth. He cursed under his breath.

"Where's he now?"

"Not here that I know of." Parker blew air across his burned tongue. "Old Gault fired him this morning."

"You don't say?"

I could see the squint in Karlin's eyes. It was probably a mannerism that meant he was thinking hard.

"The day watch said Mr. Gault got on Charles about some matter or other and Charles sassed him. The old man gave that boy an hour to get his things and leave the Farm. After that hour, the watch was told to arrest him if he came on Gault land again."

A clock struck in some distant part of the house. I checked my watch. It was three o'clock.

"I know Charles," I said. "I don't see him as the kind to kill a man he respected as much as he respected Harrison Gault." That was, of course, probably a lie. I don't think Charles respected Gault at all. He may even have hated him. But still, I didn't think he'd killed him.

"Who knows what a nigger will do when he's drunk and mad?" Karlin drank his coffee with loud, sucking noises. "You wouldn't believe me if I told you what niggers kill over."

Karlin's deputy came in, blowing on his hands. "The ambulance and the doctor finally got here." He reached for the unused mug. "I asked them if they came by way of Atlanta."

"Make that half a cup," Karlin said.

"Aw ... Andy ..." The deputy followed orders and poured half a cup.

"You know that Charles boy used to work for Mr. Gault, the one that rode that horse the last time we was here. Remember him?"

The deputy laughed. "The black cowboy? Yeah."

"Find him and bring him to the station. Try Bartha's first and then the Red Dog."

"You want him all in one piece, Andy?"

Karlin's face reddened. "Stop that joking. Some people might not understand you." His eyes cut toward me. "Don't use no force you don't have to."

"Yes, sir."

I placed my cup on the table. "I've got to call Mr. Gault's lawyer in Atlanta."

Parker said he'd go with me and he'd unlock the door so I could make the call from Gault's office.

As we left, I heard the Sheriff and his deputy joking with the cook and complimenting her on her good coffee.

CHAPTER TWELVE

I woke Frank Butler and gave him the bad news. He said he would dress and get on the road as soon as he could.

I stopped by my room to get my topcoat. I wanted to get to the Sheriff's station before they beat Charles to death.

When I returned to the hall, I could hear loud crying in the distance. I followed the sound and found myself in the rear wing where the nursery and Anna's rooms were located. The young black nurse came from Anna's bedroom and closed the door behind her. The closed door muffled the sound of the crying.

The nurse walked toward me and stopped. "Miss Anna just heard about Mr. Gault."

"You tell her?"

"I thought it was best."

It was probably true. I started for the door to her bedroom. The nurse moved over and blocked my path.

"It might be better to see her later. I just give her a shot to help her rest."

I listened. The crying appeared to grow weaker even as I stood there. "I'll see her when she's awake. Mr. Butler will be here from Atlanta by then."

I walked outside. My car was parked out front. While I waited for the engine to warm up, I walked around the side of the house. The floodlights still burned on the roof over the corral. The wheelchair and the old man's body were gone. An old black man in bib overalls was in the corral with the Morgan stud. The old man was trying to lead the horse from the corral toward the barn in the distance. The Morgan was skittish, still nervous, quivering.

I watched until the old man got the horse from the corral and led him toward the barn. Then I returned to my car and drove to the Sheriff's station.

The Sheriff's station was a squat brick building that looked like a cell block of a prison. The windows on the second floor were all barred.

A pot-bellied man in a uniform shirt that was too tight for him sat behind the desk in the entrance room. He looked up at me from his cup of coffee and his half-eaten candy bar. "I help you?"

"I want to see the Sheriff."

"He's busy now." He chewed. "You take a seat over there until…"

I heard a thump and a muffled yell. There were two doors and a staircase straight ahead. One door had lettering, SHERIFF A.W. KARLIN. The other door was not marked at all. The sound seemed to come from the room beyond the unmarked door. "He's expecting me. It's about the Gault case." I lunged for the unmarked door. The pot-bellied man was slow getting to his feet. I reached the door three steps ahead of him.

"Hey, you can't go in …"

The door wasn't locked. I swung the door open and stepped inside the room. It was small, not much bigger than a cell. Sheriff Karlin had one haunch perched on the edge of a wooden table in the center of the room. His deputy had his back to me. He was leaning over someone who was on the floor in the rear right corner of the room.

The deputy turned to see who had entered. That movement gave me a look at the man on the floor. It was Charles. He was seated there, back braced against the wall. His hands were cuffed behind him. A trickle of blood bubbled over his lower lip and ran down his chin.

"You're not wanted here," Karlin said.

The pot-bellied deputy chugged up behind me and placed a hand on my shoulder. I pushed it away.

"They read you your rights, Charles?"

Charles shook his head. Blood splattered down the front of his blue denim shirt.

"The hell we didn't." The deputy swung around toward Charles and pulled back his foot for a kick.

"I wouldn't do that," I said.

Karlin grunted. He didn't like the situation. "Willie, you back off, you hear?"

I passed the deputy and leaned down and caught Charles under the arms and drew him to his feet. He wobbled. I half-pulled, half-carried him to the chair on the other side of the table. "Get me something to clean the blood off him with."

The pot-bellied deputy trotted away and returned a minute later with a wad of wet paper towels. I stood over Charles and wiped away as much of the blood as I could.

"Read him his rights," I said.

Karlin read them one-by-one from a card he carried in his uniform shirt pocket. I had him stop after each one and make certain that Charles understood that one before I allowed Karlin to move on to the next one. At the end of the reading, I backed away from Charles. "You remember Mr. Butler, the lawyer from Atlanta, Charles? He'll be here in two or three hours. If I were you, I wouldn't talk to Sheriff Karlin until I've had a talk with Mr. Butler."

"I didn't kill Mr. Gault."

A thin ribbon of blood still ran down Charles' chin. It was probably from a cut inside his mouth.

"How about taking the cuffs off him? He's not going anywhere."

Karlin nodded at the deputy.

After the cuffs were removed, Charles pressed one of the paper towels to his mouth.

Karlin stood and rubbed the haunch that had been on the table edge. "Why'd Gault fire you, boy?"

I saw Charles jaw muscles tighten at the Sheriff's use of *boy*. He knew he was out gunned. "It was because of Miss Anna. He said it was my fault Miss Anna got the keys to that blue car of hers when he'd told her she wasn't to drive it anywhere."

"Was it your fault?" I circled the table and took out a package of smokes and offered him one. I lit mine and then his.

"I suppose it was," Charles said. "She told me all she wanted to do was drive around some to clear her head."

"And you believed her?" I watched Charles take the cigarette from his mouth and look at the end of it. There was blood on it from his mouth. He mashed the butt out in the ashtray.

"I don't think Miss Anna meant to lie to me. The way I see it, she got out on the highway and changed her mind."

"So, he fired you and you left the Farm?"

"That was this morning." Charles nodded.

"But you returned again tonight."

Sheriff Karlin's head swung toward me.

"Some of my clothes were still there."

I saw a thin smile on Karlin's face. Now he was glad he'd allowed me in the interrogation room. I was doing his work for him. "How'd you get past the security?"

"It was easy. Cold weather the guards don't do the whole rounds they're supposed to. There's a place where there's a dog hole under the fence. I got in there."

"So, you went to get your things?"

He nodded. "But I was still mad."

"When was this?"

"Just past midnight."

"Let me try a guess," I said. "You went to the barn and got the Morgan and turned him out in the corral."

"Yes, sir."

"Why?"

"I wanted Mr. Gault to get up in the morning and look out that window in his office and see that prize horse of his freezing half to death. That was because I was mad."

"Then you left?"

A nod. "I went back to Eartha's and did some drinking."

"That's where I found him," the deputy said. "That woman, Eartha, says he's been there since half past midnight. That is, the second time he was there he got there about twelve-thirty."

I mashed the last of my cigarette in the tray. I placed the remainder of my pack in front of Charles. "Let me talk to you a minute in private, Sheriff Karlin."

Karlin dipped his head toward Charles. "Put him in a cell, Willie."

"No roughhouse," I said.

"Keep your fists to yourself," Karlin said.

The Sheriff and I walked through the outer room and entered his office. Karlin sat in the swivel chair behind his cluttered desk and waved a hand toward a coffee urn that steamed and bubbled on a table to his left. "Pour us a coffee while I find the cream." He reached into the desk drawer on the bottom right.

I poured two cups and left some room at the top. I placed the cups on the desk top and watched him remove the cap from a pint of rye.

He leaned toward me. "Say when."

We drank. I could feel the morning chill leaving me.

"I used to be a cop," I said.

"Is that right?" His flat, button-like eyes regarded me sternly.

"One hundred percent the truth," I said. "The way I see this, you can get Charles on some kind of trespassing. Maybe even malicious trespassing because of what he was doing with the horse. But that's all."

"You're a corker, Hardman. I give you my best rye and you try to run a tall tale like that past me."

"I appreciate the rye." To show that I did I took a noisy swallow and smacked my lips. "You're going to have trouble convincing a jury that Charles let that Morgan in the corral with the idea, the intention, that the horse would trample Mr. Gault to death."

"Finish your coffee," Karlin said. "You don't have to hurry."

"Good jail coffee," I said. "You'll get all my business from now on."

I shivered in the chill wind that blew across the corral. Frank Butler, wearing a fur-lined coat and a shapeless tweed hat, stood beside me.

"Where was the body, Jim?"

"There, near the center of the corral." I pointed toward a spot where fresh sand had been spread. It made me think of a bullfight I'd seen in one of the border towns in Mexico, how the sand was shoveled about the ring after each bull was killed. To cover the swamp of dark blood.

"And the wheelchair?"

"A few feet this side of the new sand ... and a couple of steps to our right."

"How do you see it?"

I shook my head. "I slept through it, remember?"

"Play the game for me. Argue it for a courtroom."

I opened a new pack of cigarettes and shook out one and lit it behind cupped hands. "I'm arguing it was an accident?"

Butler's face was bland, smooth. "What else could I mean?"

"All right. During the night old Gault heard his stud out here. The room he slept in was just past that wheelchair ramp and back door. He was close enough for the noise of the Morgan to awaken him. Probably. he didn't sleep well anyway. He hears the horse and it's too close for the sound to be coming from the barn." I pointed toward the barn in the distance. "He gets out of bed and into his wheelchair, He wheels himself from his bedroom down the hall to his office. He opens the drapes at the window that overlooks the corral. Sure enough, he sees his prize stud out here in the cold. Maybe the cold wouldn't have hurt the Morgan. But old Gault is used to babying that horse. He leaves the office, goes down the hallway to the back door and outside. Down the ramp to the gate. Here's the hard part. Why does he enter the corral? Maybe he's too angry to think straight. Maybe he really believes he can enter the corral, get up out of the wheelchair and lead the stud to the barn. If that's the way he was thinking, the rest follows. He opens the gate and enters the corral. He wheels himself toward the horse. He's going to get as close as he can before he has to leave the wheelchair. Gault pushes himself closer and closer. But the Morgan is skittish. All he sees is the dark shape, this shadow, coming close to him. He's trapped and he rears up. He comes down and bumps the wheelchair. Gault falls to the ground. A hoof strikes him. Then another. In a frenzy the Morgan stomps the form on the ground until there's no movement and no sound from Gault. But now there's something new that frightens the horse. He smells the blood and he tries to kick his way out of the corral. That's how it is when the security guard passes by and hears the horse. He finds the horse trying to kick the fence down and Gault dead in the center of the corral."

"Why didn't Gault switch on the floodlights?"

I shook my head.

"Why didn't he merely call the security watch when he found the horse in the corral?"

"I don't know."

"You don't know much, do you?" Butler said.

"I know enough not to be in a dark corral with a big mean horse."

I opened the corral gate and stepped inside. The people who'd been inside after Gault's death, the security guard, the Sheriff and his deputy, the doctor and the ambulance attendants and the old black man who'd led the Morgan to the barn, all had made their marks in the earth there. Still, I could see, here and there, the remains of the tracks from the wheelchair tires. And something else. I squatted and took a closer look. Butler's pale shadow covered me as he leaned over my back.

Not many of them. Holes punched in the dirt that were deeper than the wheelchair tread.

"What are they?"

"A stick. The tip of a cane."

"Was there a cane in the corral with Mr. Gault?"

"I didn't see one," I said.

"A boot heel?"

"Small for a boot heel."

"A woman's boot?"

I stood. "Does Anna ride?"

"I don't know."

I crushed the cigarette against the sole of my shoe and field-stripped it. The tobacco and the wad of paper blew away from my fingers. "I left out one detail in my argument to the jury. It didn't fit the accident theory. You know the room you had the last time both of us were here?"

"Yes."

"I had that room last night. Somewhere around twelve-thirty-four or five I couldn't sleep and I was looking for an Alka-Seltzer. I heard somebody tiptoe past my room."

"Headed in which direction?"

"From downstairs toward the rear wing."

"Where the nursery is?"

I nodded.

"Where Anna's rooms are?"

"It could have been the nurse," I said.

"That's the likely explanation," Frank said. His voice was low and even.

I shaved and showered and dressed. I packed my few belongings. Frank Butler hadn't returned. I sat on the edge of the bed and closed my eyes.

A boot heal or the tip of a stick or a walking cane?

An old man who could still walk some might use a cane from time-to-time. Where? In his bedroom, getting from the bed to his wheelchair. From his wheelchair to his bed or to the bathroom.

I left the room and walked down the curved staircase. From there to the hallway that led to the backdoor and the ramp. The door to the bedroom was closed. I tried it. It wasn't locked. I stepped inside and eased the door shut behind me.

The bedroom smelled of harsh soap and sweat and old unwashed skin.

I switched on the overhead light. *There.* As easy as the roll of a doughnut. The umbrella stand against the wall, near the headboard of the bed. A collection of several sizes and shapes of walking sticks. I switched on the lamp beside the bed so there was better light.

Odd. The heads, the handles of all of the canes, except one, were dusty. *That* cane head was silver or pewter.

Carefully, I used a pen to hook the handle of the cane and lift it. I caught the shaft with my handkerchief. I drew the cane from the stand and held it closer to the strong lamp light. At first, I thought it was wiped clean. I flipped the cane and looked at it again. *There.* Where the silver or pewter handle joined the wooden shaft. A dark spot the size of my little fingernail. I turned the cane in my hand and held it between the strong light and my eyes. I saw what looked like a tuft of hair.

I returned the cane to the umbrella stand.

If this was the weapon used in a murder, then the metal head of the cane was once covered with blood and hairs from the victim's head.

I switched off the lamp beside old Gault's bed.

The murderer cleaned the blood and the hair from the handle, the head of the cane, and returned it to its usual place in the umbrella stand in the victim's bedroom.

I turned off the overhead light and listened at the door for a moment. I could hear no footsteps in the hallway. I opened the door and stepped into the hall. I pulled the door closed behind me and took a deep breath. I found that my handkerchief was still in my hand. I wiped my forehead.

But the murderer made one mistake. He was in a hurry.

After he cleaned the head of the cane, he returned it to the stand. What he did not figure on was that a small amount of blood had collected under the handle of the cane, at the joint where the head was bonded to the shaft. When the murderer placed the cane in the umbrella stand, tip and shaft down and handle up, the blood ran from under the handle and settled on the shaft of the cane just below that handle. And it dried there.

I returned to my room and waited for Frank Butler.

"I talked to Miss Catton." Frank Butler stood in the doorway.

I gave him my best blank look.

"The nurse," he explained. "Miss Catton said she did pass your room but it was twenty-five or thirty minutes later. According to her, it was closer to one o'clock."

"What was she doing in the hall?"

"She's here every other weekend by herself. The other nurse is off. When she has the duty, she looks in on the baby and Anna every hour."

"I don't think I'm wrong about the time."

"What time is it now?"

I crossed to the dresser where I'd placed my watch before I showered. It had stopped at 5:42. In all the confusion, after being awakened by the security guard, I'd forgotten to wind it. Most mornings that was the first thing I did after I got out of bed. "Forgot to wind it." I showed him the watch face.

"That particular watch," Butler said, "will be a bad witness in a courtroom."

"Maybe."

"Anna wants to see you."

He turned his wrist and showed me the time by his watch. I set mine to match his. I gave the stem a few twists. "I've had it up to here with Anna." I placed the blade edge of my hand at a point just above my eyebrows.

"I'll go with you."

"All right."

Down the hallway, following him, I reached the door to the nursery. I stopped and a young black woman, not the nurse, saw me and stood. The rocking chair continued to rock behind her as she brought the child to the door. She held out the baby and I looked down at him. The boy, Harry, had his father's face and his mother's hair.

"A fine-looking boy," I said.

Ahead of me, Butler reached the second door to Anna's suite, the one that led directly into the living room. He knocked and the door was opened. He stepped through the doorway.

I smiled at the girl holding the baby.

"Ain't he a doll baby?" she said.

I said indeed he was and moved away. I foot-dragged the fifty feet or so to the open door. Anna and Frank were already talking when I entered.

"... has to leave. He's due back in Atlanta this afternoon."

"But I need him here," Anna said. "I need him because..."
She broke off when she saw me.

Anna was dressed in jeans and a blue sweater. Her feet were
bare. There was a pair of slippers on the floor beside the chair
where she was seated. Her hair was mussed and she didn't appear
to be wearing makeup.

"Miami, you can't leave me now."

She got to her feet and started for me. I almost backed
through the doorway. My partial retreat made her hesitate. To
one side, where he stood, I saw Butler react to the name, Miami.
At first, he seemed puzzled. That changed after a moment and I
knew he had received some insight into our relationship.

"I have to go." I said.

"But I need you here to help me. Everything that has happened, all the men who have died, it is all my fault."

I went over the list in my head one more time.

Harry Gault in London. Yes, because his love for Anna had
triggered the jealousy and murder in Mitka.

Carl Busco with the knife in his chest in Atlanta. Yes and no.
She'd been there and there were real clouds over what had actu-
ally happened. But perhaps the killing would have taken place if
Anna hadn't been there that day.

And now old Harrison Gault.

I lit a cigarette and looked around for an ashtray. "What happened this morning. How is that your fault?"

She was crying now, huge washes of tears that streaked her
face. "If I had not asked Charles to help me get away from the
Farm, if Charles had not helped me, then Mr. Gault would not
have been angry with him and fired him. If Mr. Gault had not
made Charles leave the Farm, then Charles would not have taken
his revenge through his treatment of the horse. You see? If it had
not been for me Mr. Gault would still be alive."

It was a convincing argument. It did not, however, mention
the walking stick with the metal head.

I crossed the room and picked up an ashtray. I returned to my position near the doorway and stood there, tapping ashes from the cigarette. I didn't feel in any mood to try to comfort her. That was up to Butler. As the family lawyer, it was his business rather than mine.

Butler did just that, with all the practice of his years. It was certainly not her fault, he said. How could she know that Charles would act in such a foolish way? How could she know that Harrison Gault would risk his life in the corral, rather than calling the security guards as a sensible man would? The sad event of the day was merely the result of a number of circumstances over which no one had any control. It was not her fault. Blame the horse. Blame Harrison Gault's hard-headedness.

And on and on until Anna appeared to be convinced. The weeping subsided. Anna sniffled into a wadded handkerchief. I stubbed my cigarette. I placed the ashtray on a nearby table. I was ready to leave. I wanted some fresh air, away from this woman and all her tears and troubles.

The scene, if that was what it was, ended when the black nurse, Miss Catton, entered and stood behind me. I looked over my shoulder and saw that she carried a hypodermic needle in one hand, the point raised. "I called the doctor, Miss Anna. He said to give you another shot to calm your nerves."

"I don't want another shot," Anna shouted.

"You'd better do what the doctor says," Frank said. "It's the best thing. You don't want to get yourself upset again, do you?"

And have to go back to the institution, that was implied. Anna understood. The fight went out of her. "If he thinks it is best," she said to Miss Catton.

Frank Butler passed the nurse and gave her a covert nod. I followed him.

"When will I see you again, Jim?" Anna's red, swollen eyes burned at me.

I stopped in the doorway and touched the doorframe with one hand. "You won't."

Butler went outside to the car with me. He stood outside my door while I started the engine.

"Have you been in Harrison Gault's bedroom lately, Frank?" I asked.

"The last time I was here," he said.

"You know the umbrella stand?"

"The one with the walking sticks in it?"

I nodded. "There's one with a heavy silver or pewter head on it."

"His favorite," Butler said. "He had it made for him in a shop in Bloomsbury, in London."

"That cane's in the umbrella stand now. The odd thing is that there's a bit of dried blood and some hair at the joint, where the handle is fitted to the shaft of the stick."

"Is that so?" Butler lifted an eyebrow at me.

"And those holes near the tread of the wheelchair in the corral. I'm sure the tip of the cane will fit those holes."

"You've been playing detective."

"I had to do something. I can't sing and it's too cold to dance."

"What do you think I ought to do?"

"You're an officer of the court. That's up to you."

He took a step back from the car. I gunned the engine and got the hell away from there as if I was running for my life.

CHAPTER THIRTEEN

The next day, Gault's death was front page news. Not the biggest headline but the second largest. It was the party line the whole way. Harrison Gault had been trampled by his prize horse. The story even quoted Sheriff Karlin. He said that he did not know exactly what Mr. Gault was doing in the corral at that time. Still, Harrison Gault was known to be eccentric. There was no mention of any suspicion of foul play. No mention either of the walking cane.

I thought about calling Frank Butler and asking him what fucking kind of officer of the court he was anyway. I didn't make the call. For all I knew, he was still in Gaultsville.

To hell with it. It was none of my business if they wanted to kill each other. I was well out of it. As long as I kept my distance, as long as I stayed away from them, I had an even chance of living a few years longer than any of them.

It was the time of year that I like to call the Christmas mugging season. All the muggers who got caught would tell the police they were only doing this so they wouldn't have to face the children on Christmas with nothing under the tree for them.

Oh, poor Tiny Tim. Oh, poor Nell.

People who want to act friendly but aren't really friends give booze for Christmas. The more expensive the better, I guess. A rare scotch, an aged bourbon or a fancy brandy. Or even a case of decent wine, Never a scarf or a pair of gloves. Personal gifts call for making a choice of design or color or knowing the correct size. A Christmas booze list is easy. *These* get the good scotch, *these* the standard brands and *those* the bar brands.

It was the last week or so before Christmas and I was doing my booze list, too, when I heard a timid knock at the door. My fear was that Anna was back again.

I yanked open the door, preparing myself for the worst. It wasn't Anna. But I still felt like I'd been hit with a gut punch.

Marcy stood there, pale and shaky and shivering and looking too small and thin for her heavy coat. Her eyes were red and all cried out.

"Can I come in?"

Her voice was raw. I had no voice at all. I stepped aside and she came in. She stumbled a bit, so I took her gently by the elbow, and led her to the couch, then went back and closed the door.

"Are you okay?" I asked. "Are you sick?"

She shook her head. "Could I please have a drink?"

I went to the kitchen, poured us both a J&B, and brought her a glass. She knocked it back quickly. It wasn't like her at all. I brought over a kitchen chair and sat in front of her.

"I know you must hate me," she said, "but I had nowhere else to go."

"What's wrong?"

"I just had an abortion, Jim." Marcy looked me in the eye, as if daring me to say something cutting and cruel. "If there's a complication, an infection, over the holidays... I can't be alone now. I can't go to any of my girlfriends with this. They'd never look at me the same. I can't go home to my parents, they wouldn't understand or ever forgive me."

"What about Edward?"

"He walked out on me when I told him I was pregnant. He couldn't face me at work, either. So he up and quit. For all I know, he even left the country." Again, she gave me that look, waiting for the cut. "I wouldn't blame you if you threw me out."

I took her hand. It was ice cold. "Looks like I'm going to have a houseguest over the holidays."

I brought her suitcase in from the trunk of her Vega. By early evening, Marcy was settled into my room, fast asleep. I went to the grocery store and stocked up on food, drink and toiletries for the week. Later, when she woke up, I made her soup and that night, I slept on the couch.

The first couple of days were awkward. We didn't leave the house and the walls seemed to shrink in on us. We kept bumping into each other. We shared the space, but we didn't really talk. We were polite strangers, despite the years we'd spent together. I cooked for her and she began to get her strength and color back. We watched a lot of TV, sitting on opposite ends of my couch.

Hump called once, while she was asleep, to see if I wanted to go out to some bars and check the trim. I told him that Marcy was back, and that she wasn't feeling well, and that I was taking care of her, and that he might not hear from me for a while. He didn't ask any questions.

On the third night, I won the coin toss and got the bathroom first. On the way back to the couch, passing her in the bedroom, I said goodnight. I undressed and got into the bed I'd made for myself on the couch. I turned the TV on low and watched an old western. Marcy showered and, afterwards, started back for the bedroom, changed her mind, and came into the living room.

"Can we talk?" she said.

"Sure." I sat up, cleared a spot for her on the couch, and turned off the TV with the remote.

Marcy wore a wool robe that almost reached her ankles and her skin was scrubbed and glowing, without any makeup. I noticed how fine and light her hair was.

She sat on the far end of the couch. I could smell the soap on her. "Why are you going to all this trouble for me?"

"It's no trouble."

"You didn't answer my question, Jim."

"Say it's the season. It's a bad time of the year to be unhappy. I didn't want you here in Atlanta by yourself, certainly not in your condition. And I had my selfish reasons. I didn't want to spend Christmas alone."

Marcy shook her head. "I betrayed you and I said some awful things to you. That doesn't make you want to hurt me?"

"Hurting you isn't something I've ever wanted to do, Marcy, but I've managed to do it plenty of times anyway."

"Likewise," she said.

"A lot has happened since you left me. I realize now that we were both right that day in the car together."

"I don't understand."

"There's nice and there's ugly. I only live in the ugly because I don't trust the nice, I am always waiting for the ugly behind it to show itself. Or I don't wait and I go out looking for it, so I am never disappointed. That's no way to be happy. You live in the nice and sometimes the ugly intrudes but you never go looking for it."

"It finds me anyway."

"It finds us all, that's why none of us should be alone. But with your way of living, happiness is actually possible."

"Are you saying you're unhappy?"

"Not anymore."

"Because I got what was coming to me and I came crawling back?" There was an edge in her voice, a challenge. I didn't rise to it. She was picking a fight with herself, not with me.

"Because you knew I'd take you in, that I wouldn't think any less of you, and that I'd accept you as you are. It means you see me as a better man than I see myself."

"It always all about you, isn't it?" She was smiling, teasing me a bit. It was so good to see that smile.

I reached across the couch and took her hand. It was warm this time. "Are you back?"

I felt her stiffen, saw the smile fade. I'd ruined it. "I don't know, Jim."

"Whether you are or not, I want you to know something. I'm done with the life I've been living."

"What does that mean?"

"I'm going to find a job, one that allows me to see a lot less of the ugly."

She gave my hand a squeeze. "Merry Christmas."

"It's not Christmas yet."

"Feels like it to me."

It did to me, too.

The next day, I went on a buying frenzy at Rich's and bought her a new perfume she probably wouldn't like and a new purse and a pair of soft, black goatskin gloves. For myself, I bought a good bottle of Armagnac. If the price was any indication, it had some good ages blended in. I bought the same Armagnac for Hump and Art. I bought some toys for Art & Edna's kids. I had everything gift-wrapped. On the way home, I bought us a spindly little Christmas tree. It was all that was left. I bought some strands of glitter, some ornaments, and a string of lights.

When I got home, Marcy and I decorated the tree and I put the presents around the bottom. I stood beside her to admire our work. She saw the gifts with her name on them.

"You shouldn't have got me anything, Jim. I don't have a gift for you," she said.

"You already gave it to me. You're here." It was heavy-handed but true.

She smiled, then gestured to the tree. "You should turn on the Christmas lights to get the full effect."

I bent down to plug in the strand of lights in the tree. At that same instant, glass exploded inward from the living room window. I heard another sound. Gun fire.

Marcy screamed. I heard myself yelling with her. I tackled her behind the couch as it, too, seemed to explode.

I felt like I'd been kicked in the left shoulder. My arm went numb. Suddenly the room was dark. I guess the lamp had been hit or knocked over. I couldn't see anything but I could feel something warm on my hands. I didn't know if it was my blood or Marcy's.

"Got to call for help." I reached for the phone on the coffee table beside the couch. I fumbled with it and finally dialed the police number. I gave them my name and address and said I'd been shot and to send an ambulance.

I heard the screech of tires as a car sped away. I stood up, looked out the shattered window, and saw the flash under a street light of a black Mercedes disappearing around a corner.

I went to Marcy, who was on the floor behind the couch, which had a bullet hole in the back. Marcy was still breathing. Her breath was steady and even. From what I could see, she'd been hit in her lower, left side and there was some cuts that might have been caused by flying glass. The wound in her side was the bad one. I got a towel and tried to slow the flow of blood with pressure. I was about half-crazy with worry. I kept saying. "Hold on, Marcy," and then I heard the police cars and the ambulance approaching. I staggered to the front door and unlocked it and leaned against the door frame and waited for them.

Blood ran down my left arm and dripped on my feet.

Art Maloney showed up at the hospital and I think he might have hit me if Hump hadn't stepped between us. I would have let him hit me, too.

I was hurting but not enough. They'd pulled some glass from deep in my shoulder and the doctor was worried about possible nerve damage, but he'd stitched me up, shot me full of pain killers, and put my left arm in a sling.

"What have you done?" Art marched up to me, his flat Irish face red with rage, his hands balled into fists. "Who did you piss off that got Marcy shot?"

It could've been the coke dealers we'd burned, or friends of Busco's crew, or any number of enemies I'd made over the years. But I knew in my bones who it was. But I wasn't going to tell Art. This was my problem.

"I don't know." I said.

"Too many to fucking count, huh, Hardman?" Art said. Now I was Hardman to him, not Jim.

"Cool it, Art," Hump said.

"Or what, Hump? What?" Art got right up in his face. Hump didn't flinch or raise his voice.

"I'll shove your badge so far up your ass you'll need the surgeons here to remove it."

Things might have escalated, but Marcy's doctor came in and we all settled down like misbehaving children in front of a parent.

"Mr. Hardman?" The doctor said, eyeing the three of us sternly. "I'd like to talk with you about Miss King."

"You can say what you have to say in front of them." I said.

The doctor didn't seem to like it, like he'd tasted something sour, but he went on. "The bullet passed through her about as clean as one could hope for. We've stopped the bleeding and stitched her up. But there is also the issue of her, um, recent medical procedure. It has complicated things. I'm not sure if she will be able to have children again. She's lost a lot of blood and the risk of infection is high. She's going to need to stay here for a few days."

"Can I see her?"

"She's under sedation. You can see her in the morning."

The doctor left.

The fire seemed to have gone out of Art. He looked at me. "Was it yours?"

He'd guessed the abortion. It didn't take a deductive genius. Art had a wife and four kids and strong family values. But he was a cop, so he knew how it really was out there, too. He tried to keep his two worlds apart and I had no idea if he'd managed it or if it was a losing battle. I admired him for putting up the fight anyway.

I shook my head. "I haven't seen her in over a year."

Art put the pieces together and saw the picture. "Could the shooter be the other man?"

"He didn't care enough to stay in town and nurse her through it. He left her alone. He's not going to shoot her because she came to me."

"What are you and Hump working on? What kind of trouble are you in to?"

"Nothing," I said.

Art looked at Hump.

"You heard the man," Hump said.

"Fuck you both," Art said and he walked away, shoulders slumped. I wondered if he'd tell Edna the truth.

When Art was gone, Hump turned to me. "It was that Polish witch."

That's what I thought, too. She'd come to my house, saw me through the window with Marcy, and it infuriated her. "Can you stay here? Watch over Marcy while I check into it?"

He nodded. "You're in no shape to even tie your shoes."

❧   ❧   ❧

I took a taxi home and saw that somebody had arranged for plywood to be nailed over my shattered window. That had to be Art. I went inside. The Christmas tree was still standing but the presents were covered with shards of glass and spattered blood.

I went to the phone and called Frank Butler's office. His secretary said he was still in Gaultsville. A call to his unlisted home number got me an answering service that said he was unavailable.

I dialed the Gault Farm number. A man answered and I thought I recognized his voice. "That you, Charles?"

"Mr. Hardman?"

"Yeah, What are you doing there?"

"Mr. Butler hired me back."

"That's good news. Look, is Frank Butler there?"

"He left yesterday," Charles said.

"How about Anna? Is she there?"

"Mr. Butler and her left together."

"Going where?"

"Back to the hospital. Mr. Butler told me he thought Miss Anna still needed help."

"Which hospital, Charles?"

"Just a minute. I got it wrote down here somewhere." He was gone for a few seconds. Then he returned. "Pleasant Valley Hospital. It says here that the address is ..."

"I know where it is." I'd passed it a few times, on drives. It had a good reputation for dealing with the problems of the rich and the jaded, with nervous breakdowns and drugs and drink. It was located in DeKalb County, out past Emory University.

"Is something wrong, Mr. Hardman?"

"I don't know." I told him I'd call him back after I talked to Frank Butler. I broke the connection and sat there with my eyes closed, trying to reason it out.

I didn't like any of the possibilities that floated to the top of my mind.

One more time. I called Butler's law firm again. Still nothing heard from him. "Frankly," his secretary said, "I'm beginning to worry about him. Do you think he's had an accident?"

I told her I'd check around.

I tried his unlisted home number again. I got the same recorded message.

Pleasant Valley Hospital. That was the place to start. Was he expected there with Anna? Had he arrived?

I called the hospital and asked for Anna Gault's room. They told me they had no patient under that name.

CHAPTER FOURTEEN

The deputy in Sheriff Karlin's office in Gaultsville said the Sheriff was home for the afternoon and he couldn't be disturbed. I insisted. He insisted otherwise and we got into a long-distance shouting match before I convinced him it was important.

The deputy had the operator switch the call to the Sheriff's house.

Sheriff Karlin came on the line grumpy and angry, as if I'd awakened him from his afternoon nap.

I got his attention. Frank Butler was too important a man to be missing between Gaultsville and Atlanta. When I was through with my explanation, he had me give him the name of the hospital and he wanted the phone number for Butler's law firm in Atlanta.

"You think Frank Butler's got any rut left in him?"

"Huh?"

"You think he and that Polish woman could be shacked up in some motel between here and there?"

"That's a one in a million chance."

There was a long silence. "What do you think happened, Hardman?"

"Anything. That woman is as crazy as a shithouse rat."

"I'll start checking," he said.

I gave him my home number. "Call me when you know something."

He said he would.

I went to get myself something to drink and I noticed, beside the refrigerator, the pegboard and hooks where I kept my spare keys. Each key was tagged. The key to the back door, the key to my car and the key to Hump's place were there. My spare front door key was gone.

I knew what happened. The morning of the ice storm when I'd brought her into the house. It was a simple matter for her to palm the key while she was in the kitchen and I was in another part of the house. But that meant she was looking ahead. She wanted the key for some reason. And that was even before I threw rocks into the gears and questioned the way old Gault had died.

I got my .38 Police Positive and took a nap in my bedroom. The call from the Sheriff woke me at about noon.

It was one of those backwoods regional medical centers that are funded by mostly federal money. A fancy name for a square cinderblock building down a dead-end, dirt road just past a sawmill. The idea behind it was that if the town couldn't lure a doctor in, then a registered nurse and a L.P.N. could handle most of the illnesses and injuries. Serious cases were sent to the nearest hospital by ambulance.

The nearest hospital to the Rosewood Medical Center was in Atlanta, fifty-some miles away.

When I pulled into the dirt lot next to the medical center, I saw the Georgia Highway Patrol cruiser parked next to the lighted doorway. The moment I stepped from my car, a uniformed patrolman got out of the cruiser and met me at the entranceway.

"You got business here?"

"Sheriff Karlin called me. I'm supposed to talk to Frank Butler."

"You're...?"

"Hardman."

"He's expecting you." He put a hand on the door.

"How'd you find him?"

"I didn't. He found us. He stepped out of the wood right into the highway and flagged down my cruiser."

"How bad is he?"

"The nurse thinks he's got a concussion. Probably a busted collarbone and a broken leg. Add to that he was out in this weather for more than a day."

"How'd he walk on a broken leg?"

"Some of these little men fool you," the patrolman said.

I followed him inside. The walls of the center had been painted surgical gown green, the paint right over the grain of the cinderblocks. A nurse in her fifties sat behind a metal desk and rubbed her eyes and sipped a cup of hot tea. I knew it was tea because the tag of the tea bag still dangled over the side of the cup.

"This is Mr. Hardman," the patrolman said.

The nurse pushed her cup aside. She got to her feet with an effort. "He says he's got to talk to you. He's in pain but he won't let me give him anything until he sees you."

The patrolman stopped at the coffee pot. "Where's the ambulance?"

"It's on the way."

I followed the nurse through the doorway and into the ward. There were ten beds in a shotgun room. Five of the beds were occupied by blacks who looked like they'd been in the same car wreck or they'd been in the same fight and used tire irons on each other.

A bed near the front of the room was enclosed by screens. The nurse had me wait outside the screen while she went in. After a minute or so she returned. Her voice was a whisper. "Keep it as short as you can. He's exhausted and I want to get him sedated as soon as I can, before the ambulance arrives."

I nodded and stepped around the back of the screen. Frank Butler was wide awake and he looked angry. Maybe it was the anger that had made it possible for him to have the will to tough it out, to stand the pain. His face was scratched and cut, probably by the bushes when he'd made his way through the wood, limping and lurching and falling. His right arm was strapped flat across his chest. Even though the sheet was pulled to his waist I could see the bulk of some kind of splint that had been applied to his left leg.

"What happened to you?" Butler said, seeing my arm in a sling.

"Arm wrestling accident." He didn't need to know about Marcy. Not now, anyway. I circled the bed and stood over him. "Tell me about you, Frank."

It was Anna, of course.

He told me that Anna didn't want to return to Pleasant Valley Hospital. But he reasoned with her and thought she'd understood it was the right thing to do, for her and for Little Harry.

The first part of the drive was easy enough. Then twenty miles the other side of Rosewood, she asked him to stop the car by the side of the road so she could urinate. He tried to tell her there was a service station a few miles down the highway, but she said she couldn't wait that long. He'd pulled to the side of the road and she went into the woods and he waited. After ten minutes, he started worrying. Maybe she was trying to run away. He left the car and went looking for her.

"Catching her was like catching a mad bear," Butler said. "She had a piece of hardwood about a foot long and the first time I knew I'd caught her was when she stepped from behind a tree, at my back, and hit me in the head and flattened me."

When he was down, she hit him more times than he could count. He thought he'd even heard the bones breaking. He'd been half passed out when he heard the car start on the highway.

"What were you driving?"

"A black Mercedes sedan that belonged to Harrison Gault."

That fitted. I'd been right about the make of the car that I'd seen leaving my house after the shooting. She must have taken the gun from Gault's house before she left with Butler. He was lucky she hadn't shot him with it and beat him with a piece of wood instead.

The nurse poked her head between an opening in the screens. "Mr. Butler, I've got to ..."

"Another minute," Butler said.

The nurse shook her head and backed away.

A wave of pain shook Frank Butler. For a time, there I thought he might black out. He didn't. His eyelids fluttered, then locked open.

"I've got to warn you, Jim. Anna blames you for everything that happened to her. For finding Harry's body in London. For the trouble with Busco in Atlanta. For the time she's spent at Pleasant Valley. And now for revealing what really happened to Harrison Gault."

"What really happened?"

"I faced her with it after you left the Farm. I was bluffing about how much I knew but she didn't know that. I tore away at her until I got the truth." He lifted a hand and wiped at a film of perspiration that coated his face. "A little after midnight, she left her suite of rooms and went down to have it out with old Gault. They'd argued earlier about her running off to Atlanta and he'd been hard on her. She said she was so mad that she couldn't sleep. She looked in his room first. Usually old Gault didn't sleep much until daylight anyway. I think he was afraid if he went to sleep in the dark he'd die. Anyway, when she got to his room he wasn't there. She found him in his office and he was livid. He'd heard the horse in the corral. He'd left his bed and gone to the office and opened the drapes and saw his Morgan there in the cold. According to Anna, she tried to convince him to call the security watch. To let the watch take care of the horse. He wouldn't hear of it. He insisted that she go with him. On the way to the corral, he stopped by the bedroom and got his walking stick with the metal head. He said it was in case Charles was still there. So they went down the ramp and into the corral. It was dark and the horse was frightened. Gault got too close to the Morgan. He left the wheelchair and used the cane to support himself. The horse reared up and kicked down at Gault. A hoof struck Gault and knocked him down. Gault was yelling for Anna to help him. Instead, Anna picked up the cane and hit Gault with it time-and-time again. Until he was still. Then she calmed the horse and walked him over Gault's the body several times. Then she went inside, cleaned the cane, placed it in the umbrella stand and returned to her room and went to bed."

"Why did she do it?"

"She was tired of men controlling her life, pulling her strings, Gault most of all."

That seemed too pat to me. I didn't think she had any idea why she did it besides being crazy. The coke may have been the only thing that had kept her under control and I took that away from her.

The nurse pushed the screen aside. She carried a needle, point held high. "I'm going to give you this injection now whether you want it or not."

Butler nodded. She swabbed his left arm and inserted the needle. When she was done, she backed away. Butler waited until she'd left the enclosure of the screens. "I don't have much time. You're the one she really blames. You're the one in danger now."

I knew that.

But I also knew where she would strike. All I had to do was wait for it.

I stood near Frank Butler until his pain eased. My pain in the left shoulder was coming back and I'd left my pills at home. I was tempted to ask the nurse for a shot, too, but I couldn't afford to be knocked out.

I remained with him until the ambulance arrived. The driver said they were taking him to Georgia Baptist Hospital.

After the ambulance set out for Atlanta, I got into my car and followed. I stayed with it until we reached the Fulton County line. Then the driver put on his light and his noise maker and they pulled away from me.

I knew where Anna planned the party. And it would be soon, that night or tomorrow, because she couldn't wait much longer. She knew the police would be looking for her, if not for what she did to Marcy and Frank Butler, then for murdering Harrison Gault.

But Anna had to know that I knew she was coming for me and that I would take precautions. She'd seen the iron in my coat pocket when I thought Busco might be coming for me. I factored that into my plans.

I had a couple of beers by the front window at George's. The sky darkened and I drove home, passing Marcy's Vega, which was parked down the street.

I parked in the driveway, took out my gun from the glove box, went inside, turned on all the lights, and checked all the rooms. Nobody was home. I washed down some pain pills with a beer, made myself a ham sandwich, which wasn't easy with only one good hand.

The living room wasn't visible from the street with the plywood over the window, but some light creeped out through the kitchen. She'd know I was home if she wasn't out there, watching already.

I turned on the TV, slipped out the back door, crept through my dark backyard, and used a screwdriver I'd tucked in my sling to pry loose a few slats in my fence so I could sneak into my neighbor's yard. I moved along the side of his property, along his front hedge, and out to the street, where I slipped into Marcy's

Vega. It was cold in her car, but not as cold as it would be if I'd camped out in my backyard.

I put the gun on the passenger seat, slid down low, and waited.

It was around ten. I had the window rolled down a bit so my breathing wouldn't fog the glass. I was so cold, my teeth were chattering, but at least it kept me awake to see the black Mercedes slide past my house like an oil slick, headlights off.

Anna parked and walked back to my front door. She had a vodka bottle in one hand with a rag stuffed into the neck. I knew then that the bottle was full of gasoline.

I got out of the car, the .38 at my side, and walked up behind her on the sidewalk as she flicked open her lighter, the flame casting a glow over her. She was going to burn down my house.

"I can't figure out what I've done to you to deserve this," I said. "I helped you in London. If it hadn't been for me, you might never have come to this country."

Anna turned around slowly. She was dressed all in black, a black watch cap that was pulled down to cover part of her face, a black raincoat and black trousers. She had a lit lighter in one hand and a Molotov cocktail in the other as she came towards me down my front walk.

"I would have come in my own time with Mitka. I loved her. But you took her away from me, Miami. You destroyed everything when you found Harry's body."

So that was what Mitka's letter was about, I thought. Anna and Mitka were lovers. Harry and his money and the baby were just a means to an end. But then I showed up. She was right, I did ruin everything. At least now I understood her hatred of me and of men.

"Put down the bottle and the lighter, Anna. It's over."

She continued to advance towards me. "It was over for me when I lost Mitka. Now I will burn you the way you set fire to my dreams."

I raised my .38 Police Positive. "Stop or I'll put you down."

She laughed at me. "You won't shoot me, Miami. I'm a woman."

Anna touched the flame to the rag and it ignited. She pulled back her arm to throw the bottle at me.

There was a gun blast. The Molotov cocktail exploded in her hand and Anna became a fireball, totally enveloped in flames.

Her scream was inhuman, something wretched and horrible. There was a second gun blast and she fell dead, her body still aflame, onto my cold, wet lawn.

I hadn't fired a single shot.

Hump emerged out of the darkness beside me holding an ornate, double barrel shotgun, a silly Austrian hunting weapon he'd been given as a gift by his fans on Hump Evans Appreciation Day, a year after he hurt his knee and had to leave the NFL. I had no idea that he was there or that he was shadowing me.

"I would have shot her," I said.

"I know, so that's why I did it. You don't need that cloud hanging over you and Marcy forever."

"What about you?"

"All I have are clouds. I don't mind one more. Consider it your Christmas present."

And as I looked at Anna's burning corpse, and heard the sirens coming, and saw the lights going on in the houses up and down the street, I realized I'd completely lost track of the days.

It was Christmas Eve.

I called in my marker with Frank Butler at the start of the new year. He got me a job as an insurance investigator at a big firm in

Atlanta. It was ironic, since I'd often pretended, in the course of my old work, to be an insurance investigator and once had some phony cards made up. I still have one of those cards in my wallet as a reminder of my past life.

The job was dull, and the hours were long, and I had to wear a jacket and tie, but that was fine. Nobody wanted to shoot me, stab me, or set me on fire, at least not yet.

I sold my house and moved into Marcy's place at the Mellon Heights Apartments.

I lost weight, cut down on my drinking, and felt a tingle of feeling coming back in my left shoulder.

Marcy and I got married that summer in a civil ceremony in a judge's chambers. The ceremony was attended by Hump, Art Maloney and his wife Edna. The reception was held at George's Deli. Sam went all out, every deli meat and salad you could imagine and all the beer we could drink, and he hovered over Marcy like she'd just been crowned the Queen of May.

Marcy was beautiful and had a glow about her that seemed almost ethereal.

Hump sat in our favorite booth. I think it was maybe the second or third time I'd ever seen him wear jacket and a tie. But from the expression on his face, he seemed like a man attending a funeral, not a wedding. I brought two mugs of beer over to the booth and joined him.

"You look thirsty," I said.

"I am." He picked up the mug and practically swallowed the whole thing in one gulp. "I'm happy for you, Jim."

"So why do you look like you're at a wake?"

He shrugged his huge shoulders. "I can't do the nine-to-five, or stop chasing trim, or drink light beer."

"Nobody is asking you to."

Hump tipped his head to Marcy, who was laughing over something with Art and Edna and a half-dozen of her girlfriends from the office. "Marcy is going to see me as a bad influence. She's always going to be afraid I'll pull you back down into the muck."

"You're wrong about Marcy and how she feels about you. She'd trust you with our baby."

Hump looked at me over the rim of his beer mug. "What baby?"

I smiled at him. "The wedding was kind of a rush job."

Now he broke into a smile. "If it's a boy, gonna name him Hump?"

"A name like Hump Hardman would pretty much doom the kid."

"Hell, he's doomed anyway," Hump said. "What kind of father are you gonna be?"

"Old, fat and happy," I said.

A LOST HARDMAN FOUND
BY LEE GOLDBERG

D on't feel bad if you've never heard of Ralph Dennis. His twelve Hardman novels, originally published with numbered titles like *Hardman #1: Atlanta Deathwatch*, were all released in paperback in the mid-to-late 1970s by Popular Library, which packaged them as cheap, sleazy, men's action adventure novels. Most of the books in the genre were disposable hack work, slim volumes full of violence and sex with titles like *The Butcher* and *The Penetrator*, that were doomed to a short shelf life and oblivion. But the Hardman novels were something different, terrific crime novels with nuanced characters, strong plots, a remarkable sense of place and something meaningful to say about race relations in the deep south. Even so, the novels slipped into obscurity and Ralph never achieved the recognition or success he deserved, despite publishing three standalone novels outside of the series (which attracted even less attention than his *Hardman* books)

At the time of his death in 1988, Ralph was a destitute alcoholic, sleeping on a cot in the backroom of George's Deli in Atlanta and working as a clerk at a used bookstore.

But Ralph wasn't entirely forgotten. His Hardman series remained beloved by crime writers, like novelist Joe R. Lansdale (*Hap & Leonard*) and screenwriter Shane Black (*Lethal Weapon*), who credited Ralph for inspiring their work and who passionately recommended the yellowed, hard-to-find paperbacks to their friends. And that's how I discovered Ralph. A friend made me read him and I got hooked bad.

It became an expensive obsession that led me to acquire the copyright to all of Ralph's work, published and unpublished, from his estate and to co-found a publishing company, Brash Books, just to get the novels back into print.

Once I secured the rights, the attorney for the estate sent me a box of Ralph's typewritten, manuscripts, some that were published as novels and others that had never sold. I hoped there would be a long-lost Hardman among the manuscripts, but there wasn't. Or so I thought...

I also tracked down another box of Ralph's unpublished manuscripts, which one of his old drinking buddies in Chapel Hill had kept in his attic for decades. Sadly, this trove didn't include a lost Hardman, either. But there was plenty of other gold.

Over the next few years, I republished all twelve of the Hardman novels, his three standalone novels (*The War Heist* (aka *MacTaggart's War*), *The Broken Fixer* (aka *Atlanta*) and *A Talent for Killing* (aka *Dead Man's Game*) and then began releasing his previously unpublished work (like *The Spy in a Box* and *Dust in the Heart*).

All of this time spent on Ralph's work made me eager to learn more about him. I knew Ralph was a student, and later an instructor, at the University of North Carolina at Chapel Hill during the 1960s. So in the summer of 2019, I went to Chapel Hill to read through Ralph's papers at the UNC library, to meet some of his old drinking buddies, and to see the places mentioned in his books.

On the flight to North Carolina, I began reading Ralph's unpublished novel *The Polish Wife*, which was one of the manuscripts I'd received from the estate. It was about a disbarred lawyer-turned-Atlanta lobbyist named Thad Morris who gets hired by a lawyer, Frank Butler, to go to London to find a missing man. I immediately noticed some striking similarities between *The Polish Wife* and a Hardman novel.

First off, *The Polish Wife* was written in what was unmistakably Hardman's first-person voice. Or was this just Ralph's voice? Thad frequented George's Deli in Atlanta, just like Hardman. But so did Ralph, who liked to write at a table there. Was this just another friendly nod to his favorite watering hole?

Thad had a white, womanizing employee, Bill Testman, who did dirty jobs for him... and behaved and talked like Hardman's black friend Hump. Was this just Ralph's idea of a little in-joke? (C'mon, *Testman*? Really?)

Thad was a disbarred lawyer. Hardman was an ex-cop. Were they the same character? Or was Ralph just interested in characters who were outcasts from their professions?

And, finally, Frank Butler, the lawyer who hired Thad, was a character who'd appeared in *The Buy Back Blues*, the final Hardman novel. There was no question that Butler was the same character. Their backstories were identical. Did Ralph just like Butler so much that he decided to use him again in a new book?

That left me puzzling over the big question: Was *The Polish Wife* actually a rewrite of an abandoned Hardman novel? In other words, was this the long-lost Hardman novel that I'd dreamed of finding?

Even if it *wasn't,* would I be going too far, and taking too many creative liberties, if I revised it into a Hardman novel *anyway*? I certainly had the legal right – I obtained the copyright to the manuscripts specifically so I would have the freedom to make any revisions I thought were necessary – but should I do it just because I could?

There was a precedent for it. I'd substantially revised *MacTaggart's War, Atlanta* and *Dead Man's Game* before republishing and retitling them... but not to the extent that I was considering with this manuscript. In those cases, what I did was mostly editing. This time, I was contemplating a major rewrite.

I was still wrestling with this issue when I arrived in Chapel Hill, set aside the manuscript, and began going through Ralph's papers. After a few days, I came across a collection of letters that he wrote in 1976 to Wesley H. Wallace, chair of UNC's Film and Television Department, where Ralph had taught screenwriting.

That was the year that Ralph scored a contract to write his first hardcover novel, *MacTaggart's War*, a heist story set during the early days of World War II. Churchill is certain a Nazi invasion was imminent, so he sends all of England's gold to Canada for safekeeping... unaware that a group of American soldiers is waiting there to steal it all.

It was a great idea for a novel and Ralph was convinced this was going to be his break-out book that would finally make him a big-time, hardcover novelist. The story was based on a true bit of history, so Ralph spent some of the advance from his publisher on a research trip to England.

But it was an expensive trip, and Ralph's desire to stay in London a while longer, and perhaps also see more of Europe, prompted him to come up with a surprising way to make some fast cash, which I discovered in a series of handwritten letters to Wesley Wallace from London. The first was dated December 16, 1976. This line jumped out at me:

"I may do a *Hardman in London* for some extra money. I can do it while I'm doing the research for the real project."

It was soon followed by another letter to Wallace, dated January 10, 1977, that also mentioned the book:

"If I can find a typewriter, I might write a quick *Hardman in London* and put that money aside for a trip to Italy and France after I'm finished with the big book. I can probably write the *Hardman* during the later afternoon hours after I return from research."

And one more on April 27, 1977, where there was this aside:

"The lady from Atlanta is arriving in London on May 5th. A week in London, and then we head to Ireland for ten days or two weeks. The book limps along. I hope to have the first draft done by the time I leave for Ireland. If not, I'll have to take a few pads with me to do some early morning writing while the lady gets her beauty sleep."

Holy crap.

Now I was certain that *The Polish Wife* was once *Hardman in London*. Either Popular Library had passed on the book, or Ralph had second thoughts about doing another Hardman. Whatever the reason was, at some point, he must have decided to revise *Hardman in London* into a standalone by simply changing the names and a few minor story points. (It didn't work. The book never sold. In fact, *MacTaggart's War,* released in 1979, was the last book by Ralph published in his lifetime).

The letter was "the smoking gun" I needed to justify to myself revising *The Polish Wife* back into a Hardman novel.

So that's what I did. Thad Morris reverted to Jim Hardman. Bill Testman reverted to Hump. Thad's secretary Gail reverted to Marcy, etc. But the revision wasn't as simple as merely doing a search-and-replace for names. I had to undo the rewriting Ralph had done to make Hardman into a disbarred-lawyer-turned-lobbyist instead of an ex-cop-turned-unlicensed-detective. I also had to undo some other plot and character points that didn't align with the Hardman series.

I was working with Ralph's rough, typewritten manuscript, so I also did extensive editing, rearranging some scenes and chapters and deleting about 12,000 words. In the end, I'd say ninety percent of *All Kinds of Ugly* is written in Ralph's own words.

It was an honor and a thrill to discover and publish one, last Hardman novel. But it's also bittersweet for me because there's no doubt this is truly the final book. The ending makes that clear. And yet, it feels good knowing that Ralph saw an end, and a future of sorts, for his characters and wrote it, even if we never got a chance to read it in his lifetime.

At least, we can read it now.